THE NILE ADVENTURES

THE CROCODILE CURSE

SAVIOUR PIROTTA

ILLUSTRATED BY
JO LINDLEY

Books by Saviour Pirotta

Set in Ancient Egypt:

THE NILE ADVENTURES

The Heart Scarab

Set in the Stone Age:

THE WOLFSONG SERIES

The Stolen Spear

The Whispering Stones

The Mysterious Island

The Wolf's Song

Set in Ancient Greece:

ANCIENT GREEK MYSTERIES

Mark of the Cyclops

Secret of the Oracle

Pirates of the Poseidon

Shadow of the Centaurs

Set in the Islamic Golden Age:

The Golden Horseman of Baghdad

THE CROCODILE CURSE

For my mum, Giorgia Pirotta - S.P.

The Nile Adventures: The Crocodile Curse
An original concept by author Saviour Pirotta
© Saviour Pirotta, 2022

Illustrations by Jo Lindley
© Jo Lindley, 2022

Published by MAVERICK ARTS PUBLISHING LTD
Studio 11, City Business Centre, 6 Brighton Road,
Horsham, West Sussex, RH13 5BB
+44 (0) 1403 256941
© Maverick Arts Publishing Limited August 2022

A CIP catalogue record for this book is available
at the British Library.

ISBN: 978-1-84886-894-6

CONTENTS

The Crocodile on the Riverbank

Adapted from a 3000-year-old Ancient Egyptian
poem discovered on an earthenware pot.

My friend waits over there,
On the other side of the river.
I would like to visit her
But the river is in flood
And a crocodile lies waiting,
A stock-still guard on the riverbank.
Still, I wade into the water.
Why is it that friendship makes us do
brave things?
Turns the stormy water into a balmy field
under our feet?

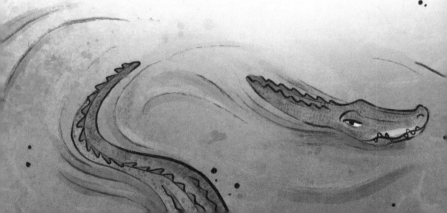

The thought of meeting my friend guides me
across the river,
Toes holding firmly in the sand.
Her spell has made the crocodile fall asleep.
Where is she?
Ah there she is,
Waiting.
Smiling.
She is the queen of the river.

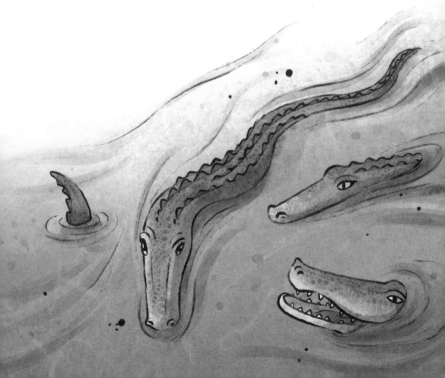

Prologue

General Tatia stood motionless, his hands hanging by his sides as if he were still a foot soldier in a military parade. Dim moonlight bathed his face, but the general knew this was not the same moon that shone down on the Black Land. He was not alive. He was dead. He had travelled through the stars in his barque and now he had descended to the gloomy underworld, the place all Egyptians feared and called the Duat.

The forty-two god-judges hovered in a wide circle around him. He could not see their faces, only their golden eyes blinking rapidly in the darkness. He felt like he was surrounded by lions or tigers ready to pounce, but he had no idea if they were tame pets or wild beasts.

These judges, the assessors of Ma'at, would decide if he deserved to move on to the place they called Aaru, the glorious Field of Reeds—a happy, sunny world where he would be reunited with his friends and loved ones. Or they might decide he had led a bad life, and he would be gobbled up by the monster-goddess Ammut.

The judges' voices echoed around the general.

"He has answered all our questions correctly…"

"It seems he has never robbed," growled a deep voice.

General Tatia had studied the Scroll of Coming Forth By Day and knew this was Fire-Embracer speaking. He was the god whose job was to determine if the man standing before him had ever stolen from a temple or public building.

Another judge stepped into the pale light

surrounding the general and looked him straight in the eye. He was Nosey One, tasked with finding out if the recently deceased had ever stolen from his fellow men. "Never cheated anyone out of as much as a loaf of bread," he declared.

"But I deduce from his answers to my questions that he lied many times," said another judge, who was called Flame. "That weighs heavily against him."

"And he quarrelled," cut in another judge, called You-of-the-Darkness. He hovered into the light so that the general saw a round face, with kohl-ringed eyes. "He fought with his friends, with his wife, even with Pharaoh himself. He quarrelled a lot."

"He got some of the answers to our questions wrong too," whispered another judge, as You-of-the-Darkness stepped back into the shadows and she took his place in front of Tatia.

Others agreed with her.

"And some answers he only got right because

of the spells inscribed inside his tomb."

"Or written in the costly spell book which the priests placed in his coffin. The spells worked magic on his tongue so that he only said what we wanted to hear."

The gods' whispers floated around Tatia, spinning a web of fear around him. There were so many judges talking over one another, it was impossible to tell who was saying what.

"But his answers showed us he also lived his life well," cried You-of-the-Darkness.

"Yes, he lived according to the gods' rules and wishes. He behaved better than any other general we have judged recently."

Another goddess, known as White of Teeth seemed to take Tatia's side. "He was kind too, by my reckoning. His heart positively overflowed with charity."

"But also, I find, he was often unnecessarily harsh," said a judge with a soft voice. Tatia was sure this was Water-Smiter.

Another god, Over-the-Old-One, spoke up. His role was to find out if Tatia had ever scared or bullied people. "Yes, I thought so too. Cruel, I would say. Especially with the weak! The poor and the slaves."

"But perhaps not that cruel," argued the goddess, Nefertem. "He punished but not severely. I would say he was like most people of his class. He expected the best from himself and the best from those he owned or employed."

"Yes," replied a judge called Owner-of-Faces. "He couldn't abide people disobeying. His word was law."

"Perhaps that is why Pharaoh made him a general in the first place," suggested Disturber. "A general must have the respect of his soldiers..."

You-of-the-Darkness tutted angrily. "If we judge him as harshly now as he judged others during his lifetime..."

The muttering continued, spinning the web of fear into a tight cocoon around the general. His *ghostly dog, his most loyal pet who had journeyed with him on the barque, whimpered by his feet. He too was scared; his eternal fate rested entirely in his master's hands. If the general made it to the Field of Reeds, his dog would live on forever by his side. But if the general failed, the dog would be devoured by Ammut with him.*

Suddenly, the whispering stopped. The god Anubis stepped forward, the dreaded scales of justice dangling from his right hand. The general had only ever seen pictures and statues of the jackal-headed god before. In those, he always looked scary. Now, holding the scales up high, he was absolutely terrifying to behold. He towered over the general, a true giant. His massive teeth were sharper than any jackal's the general had ever seen.

"Behold, the feather of Ma'at," he growled. An ostrich feather fluttered out of the darkness to settle in one of the scale's pans.

Like all the people in the Black Land, the

general knew that Ma'at was the goddess of order, truth and justice. This feather was a symbol of all the ideals she embodied, the rules she wanted all humans to obey.

"And behold," roared Anubis. A flashing, bright-red object appeared on the palm of his left hand. General Tatia knew this was his own heart. It was going to be weighed against Ma'at's feather and, if it was found that the general's misdeeds had made it heavier, he would be refused entry to the Field of Reeds. The general's hand flew to the heart scarab amulet at his chest. He prayed it would work its magic; its power would prevent his heart from giving away his past mistakes.

The ghostly dog whimpered as Anubis carefully laid the heart on the scales. For one horrific moment, the pan dipped lower than the one with the feather. The general tightened his grip on the heart scarab, his lips mouthing a silent prayer, and the pan started rising back.

The general could hardly watch. Would it rise

enough to save him? A gasp rippled through the circle of judges. The two pans were dangling neck and neck. Neither one was higher nor lower than the other.

"A dilemma," hissed Flame. "The general has not lived a good enough life to merit him travelling on to the Field of Reeds."

"And yet he has not been bad enough for his soul to be fed to Ammut," said Far-Strider.

Ammut, the demon-goddess—part lion, part hippo and part crocodile—was lurking nearby in the gloom. She gnashed her teeth hungrily.

"What shall we do?" asked Flame. "This has never happened before…"

As if in answer, a shower of stars cascaded behind Anubis. They swirled and clustered together and out of the dazzling light stepped a tall, regal figure with powerful wings on her back. Her eyes, thickly lined in black, looked kindly at General Tatia.

"I am Ma'at," she said, "daughter of the great

Amun-Ra and Hathor. The goddess of truth, justice, order and balance."

A second figure appeared behind her, tall and with the head of an ibis. "This is my husband, Thoth, the god of writing and wisdom," said Ma'at. "You have offered sacrifice to me all your life, General Tatia. You have also been a loyal friend to Pharaoh, whom I protect with my most special magic. That is why I have come to your rescue."

The goddess turned to the judges. "You cannot decide if this man should go to the Field of Reeds or be condemned to wander the Duat forevermore. I have a solution in mind. You are not sure if the general has been cruel or kind during his life. We shall send his ka on a mission that will prove he can be kind. If he succeeds, his heart will weigh lighter than my feather of truth. Do you all agree?"

A murmur of approval ran through the judges.

"We are only minor gods and you have power

over us, oh great and holy Ma'at," declared Nosey One. "We shall gladly do as you say."

The goddess turned to Tatia. "General, you have often threatened others with violence and punishment. Now it is time to show kindness, and you must do it humbly. The Black Land is in grave danger..."

Ma'at whispered in the general's ear and his eyes grew wide with horror. Then she held up an ankh, the symbol of life.

"This powerful symbol will protect you on your mission, General Tatia. My power, and that of Thoth, will go with you. You'll need it."

1

Pharaoh Visits His Tomb
- Renni -

Renni peered out of Ramesses's tomb in the Valley of the Kings, the arid land where many pharaohs and other important citizens of the Black Land were buried. The afternoon sun was blinding but he could see a colourful line of people winding their way across the hot desert sand. His breath caught in his throat. Pharaoh Ramesses was coming to inspect his unfinished tomb. Would he be satisfied with everything he saw? Renni had heard that Ramesses was incredibly difficult to please. Perhaps that was because pharaohs were part-god. Would he like the paintings Renni had helped paint on the walls?

Renni's Uncle Pepy, who was his teacher and mentor, pulled him gently back. "Renni, come stand beside me. And do as I do when the royal retinue approaches. Don't forget, you must never look Pharaoh in the eye."

"But I've looked at Pharaoh before," said Renni, thinking back to the time he, his elder brother, Mahu, and their friend, Princess Balaal, had attended the Beautiful Festival of the Valley. They were in the middle of a dangerous adventure then, but Renni, like everyone else in the crowd, had feasted his eyes on Ramesses—the most glorious Pharaoh the Black Land had ever seen.

"Pharaoh was making a public appearance then," replied Uncle Pepy. "He was there as a king and a god. You were allowed to look at him just as you are allowed to look on the statues of the gods during a festival. Today he's here in a personal capacity, as a holy man who wants to make sure his tomb is perfect and that nothing will ruin his chances of uniting with Amun-Ra when he dies.

We must treat him with respect."

As he spoke, the royal party approached the open tomb. First came a double line of slaves, all dressed immaculately in white. Even though they were slaves, their arms jingled with expensive bracelets. Golden collars studded with precious stones flashed round their necks. They reminded Renni of the bejewelled cats he had once seen in a rich woman's mansion: dressed to impress but ultimately prisoners for life.

Following the slaves came a group of important people, the men in stiff linen kilts and flowing robes. Like the women who walked by their sides, they wore elaborate makeup. Their cheeks were tinted with red powder, their fingernails painted a bright orange. Lashings of thick, black kohl ringed their eyes. Renni knew the eye makeup wasn't there just to make them look good. It helped protect their eyes from the harsh sunlight.

Behind the noblemen walked a small crowd of children in white, pleated kilts. Like Renni, the younger ones wore their hair in a sidelock. The boys' chests were festooned with amulets in the shape of the Eye of Horus. The girls wore clean linen robes tucked in at the waist. They had beads sewn to the hem of their dresses, which tinkled as they walked.

Renni knew by their proud looks that these were some of Pharaoh's many children. Their nurses walked respectfully behind them, carrying flasks of water and baskets of fresh fruit. Male slaves fanned them with peacock feathers.

Following the children came Pharaoh himself, carried in a litter by muscular soldiers.

His long, handsome face shone like polished copper in the hot sun, but Renni was disappointed to see he was not wearing the double crown of the Black Land. Instead, Pharaoh wore a thick black wig, which hid his famously red hair.

A young priest trotted beside him, holding a deerskin umbrella to shield him from the sun. To Renni's relief, there was no sign of the infamous vizier who usually accompanied Pharaoh wherever he went.

Paser, the old vizier, was an ambitious and cruel man who would stop at nothing to get what he wanted. Rumour had it that he had fallen gravely

ill after eating spoiled catfish. He was unable to leave his beautiful mansion by the Nile, not even to go to court or the temple. It was said that he was surviving on a few drops of homemade magic potion every day.

Renni knew the rumours were probably all lies. The vizier was in hiding because he was angry. Angry that he had not managed to steal his old enemy General Tatia's heart scarab! Renni, Mahu and Balaal had seen to that in a breathless adventure that could have cost them their lives.

Renni shivered just thinking about the old vizier. What was he up to now that his evil plans had been thwarted? Was he thinking up new mischief?

"Look, what did I tell you? Pharaoh is not wearing his false beard today," whispered Uncle Pepy as the gold-encrusted litter stopped outside the tomb. "And he does not carry the sacred crook and whip. That means His Majesty is here as a person, not as a god. Just as I thought."

"Behold Pharaoh," announced the priest holding the umbrella. "Behold the keeper of harmony and balance, elect of Amun-Ra."

Uncle Pepy nudged Renni and threw himself face down on the ground. Renni followed, as did all the other artists and craftsmen.

"We humbly pay our respect to Pharaoh," said Uncle Pepy loudly on behalf of all the workers gathered outside the tomb.

"Come, get to your feet, all of you," said Pharaoh as the soldiers set down his litter. He smiled at Uncle Pepy. "And how are you today, Master Painter?"

"I am well, Your Majesty," replied Uncle Pepy, keeping his eyes down.

"Come, come," said Pharaoh, "you may look upon my face. Today I am here as a mortal."

Pharaoh turned to Renni, whose heart nearly stopped in his chest.

"And this is…?"

"My nephew, Renni, Your Majesty. He is my

apprentice and has done excellent work on your tomb."

"Well done, young one," said Pharaoh. "Keep working hard and no doubt you will be as much in demand as your uncle one day."

"Yes, Your Majesty. Thank you, Your Majesty," Renni managed to blurt out. He kept his eyes lowered, but he was aware of the princes and princesses glowering at him. Renni was friends with a princess: the princess Balaal, who was a daughter of a Fenkhu king in the north! Balaal was resourceful, clever and fearless. She did not stand on ceremony. These royal children seemed to be very different. 'Haughty' was the word that came to mind.

"Lead on, Master Painter," said Pharaoh. "Let me see how the paintings in my tomb are coming along."

"Father, let me walk with you!" One of the princes stepped up to Pharaoh. He looked slightly older than Renni's brother, Mahu. Thin as a stick, he still sported a curly sidelock that cascaded down to his shoulder. Gold rings woven into it flashed in the sunshine. He had smiley eyes.

"This is my fourth son, Khaemwaset," announced Pharaoh with obvious pride in his voice. "We call him Khaem for short. He has a good heart. He was born to become a priest of Ptah if his passion for history does not get in the way." Pharaoh looked to Khaem with a raised eyebrow. "My son loves nothing better than exploring crumbling ruins and trying to imagine new uses for them. What fantastical stories will you come up with after exploring my magnificent new tomb, I wonder, Khaem?"

Prince Khaem cleared his throat. "I do admit I like history and art," he explained. "And when I grow up, I will have all the fallen buildings in the Black Land repaired and restored to their former glory."

"And no doubt you shall discover who owned them and lived in them too," cut in one of the prince's sisters.

"Yes, and I shall have their names carved in the walls so that they will never be forgotten again," replied Prince Khaem fiercely.

Pharaoh smiled at Uncle Pepy. "There is a fire inside this boy. If only it could burn just as brightly for his priesthood. But enough of idle talk. Lead the way, Master Painter. Let us have a look at your work."

Renni followed the royal party nervously. He was proud of Uncle Pepy's skills and satisfied with his own contribution to the project, but it was always difficult when people looked at your work for the first time. And when it was Pharaoh himself judging it… Renni had no words. He fingered the amulet in his sidelock, praying that

Ramesses would approve of his work.

Men with flaming torches came forward to illuminate the walls. Pharaoh tilted his head up and clasped his hands behind his back as he walked up and down the corridor, inspecting the pictures. Several princes and princesses did the same, walking in a tight group around him. They reminded Renni of goslings imitating their mother.

Pharaoh stopped in front of the main picture. It showed him in a dramatic battle scene, riding a chariot pulled by his favourite horse. The ground around him was littered with the bodies of fallen enemy soldiers. Vultures swooped down from the sky, hungry for human flesh.

Renni loved this piece of work and had looked upon it many times. It was his favourite in the whole tomb so far. But would Pharaoh agree?

There was a long moment of agonising silence as the entire royal party studied the picture. Then Pharaoh threw a sideways glance at Prince

Khaem, inviting his opinion.

"It's magnificent," declared the prince softly. "Look how well the Master Painter drew your face, Father. Most artists just draw what they have been taught, without much thought. But this work is different. It looks… *alive*."

"You are right, Khaem," agreed Pharaoh. "This is good work." He turned to Uncle Pepy. "Well done, Master Painter. You have done us proud."

Prince Khaem smiled at Renni. "And well done to you too," he said. "I can't tell which is your uncle's work and which is yours. The gods have blessed you with a rare talent."

Renni felt a lump in his throat. Never in his life had anyone praised him so highly.

"Thank you, Your Highness," he murmured, bowing deeply. "I am indeed indebted to the gods for their generosity."

"I think, Renni, you are only a few years younger than me," said Prince Khaem. "Perhaps, when I am old enough to travel around our beautiful and sacred country, you can be my travelling companion. You can decorate the old temples and buildings that I rebuild. We might even explore the ancient pyramids together."

"My nephew would be proud to act as your painter," said Uncle Pepy on behalf of Renni, who seemed to have lost the use of his tongue with astonishment. He—Renni, from the poor side of Waset—travelling with and working for a prince of the royal house of Kemet? Surely, he was fast asleep and dreaming…?

"Come and see me at the palace tomorrow," said Prince Khaem. He took a ring off his finger and handed it to Renni. It was a large silver ring, decorated with a blue carving of a frog. "Show this to the guards and they will let you in. I have been working on a picture to decorate my library wall. It shows the god Thoth inventing writing. I would appreciate your opinion of it."

"Thank you, Your Highness," said Renni. He almost put the ring on his finger, then thought twice about it and stowed it away carefully in his bag. He didn't want to risk losing it or, worse, having it stolen on the streets.

Prince Khaem was about to speak again when Pharaoh put up a hand to stop him. He was staring straight ahead at the late afternoon sunlight, which was now filling the corridor.

"Could it be…?" he muttered, hurrying to the entrance.

The priest who'd been holding Pharaoh's umbrella hurried after him. "Your Majesty, what is the matter?"

Pharaoh stopped at the entrance to the tomb. "I can't believe I got the measurements wrong," he gasped. "The rays of the setting sun are not reaching directly into my tomb."

Renni knew what Ramesses meant. It was very important that sacred buildings were correctly aligned with the sun and the stars. It's how their light shone on Pharaoh's coffin when he died, filling it with their magic. Pharaoh himself took the measurements for new temples and tombs, which were grand ceremonies attended by the most powerful people in the land.

"Summon the Master Builder and Master Architect at once," Ramesses ordered the young priest. "I regret this entrance will have to be *moved!*"

2

Feeding the Ibis
- Mahu -

Mahu lay stretched out on his back, his eyes shut tight against the afternoon sun. It might be the season of the great flood but it was still fiercely hot. It was always hot in the Black Land, unless you went north. Mahu had heard that it was often cool where the land met the open sea. Sometimes it even rained in the hot season. *Imagine standing in an open field,* Mahu thought, *and letting cool, clear water run down your face and back. Water that you hadn't pumped out of the ground yourself!*

Mahu's skiff bobbed on the water of Iteru, the Great River. He'd tied it to a tree so it wouldn't get carried away by the current. The stretch of sand where he usually kept his boat was underwater.

Since his father, a gilder, had died, it had fallen on Mahu to provide for his mother and younger brother Renni. And the only way he could do that was by working in the fields, which were currently submerged under flood water. When the water receded, it would leave a rich layer of mud, perfect for growing crops. Mahu would be digging, hoeing and planting from dawn until well after dusk.

Mahu sighed. He was a good farmer but his heart wasn't in it. His dream was to become a sailor. But a poor person without connections or influential friends could only join a crew if he bribed the boat captain with a gift. Mahu didn't have anything to give.

He thought bitterly about the time he'd tried to get his hands on a suitable present for a captain. To pay for it, he'd forced his younger brother, Renni, to steal a piece of treasure from a general's tomb. Except Renni had pinched a heart scarab by mistake and the *ka* of its owner, a dead general, had come after them.

Mahu, Renni and their friend, Princess Balaal, had found themselves in the thick of an adventure that had brought them into great danger. Mahu knew he would never put them through that again, no matter how badly he wanted to make his dream come true.

Still, Mahu reckoned, one day he would join a ship and sail on the great, wide sea. Not even the gods could stop you achieving your ambition if you put your mind to it.

There was a disturbance in the water as a flock of birds landed close to Mahu's boat. He sat up, expecting to see crocodiles snapping their powerful jaws. The crocodiles got fat at this time of year, finding easy pickings among the fish, birds and people displaced by the flood.

Surprisingly, there were no crocodiles. The birds were ibises, with long beaks that curved downwards and small, beady eyes. The feathers on their heads and necks were a sooty black, but their wings glowed a bright white.

With the riverbank underwater, Mahu realised the poor creatures could not find any crabs to eat. He fished in his bag for a stale piece of bread and broke it into pieces before tossing it into the water.

The ibises swooped on it, grunting and smacking their long beaks.

One of them turned to Mahu and fixed him with a red-ringed eye. For a moment, he had the horrifying impression that the eye was human... that he had seen it somewhere before. Then the moment passed. The ibis blinked and looked away.

I'm going mad, thought Mahu. *Boredom is sending me round the bend. I need to get my hands on a gift for a captain, fast.*

3

An Audience with Prince Khaem
- Renni -

"It is such a shame that you will have to repaint your beautiful pictures from scratch," said Prince Khaem as a servant placed a cup in front of Renni. "Do you take honey and cinnamon with your goat's milk?"

"Yes, please," said Renni. He'd never tasted cinnamon before, a spice only the very rich could afford. He took a sip of the drink, which was sweet and delicious. "It is a shame," he agreed with Prince Khaem, "but it is also an opportunity to paint even better pictures. There were a lot of things I didn't like about my work."

"I like your way of thinking," said the prince.

"Always trying to do better." He sipped his own drink thoughtfully.

Renni looked around him. Earlier that morning, he had presented himself at one of the many servants' entrances in Pharaoh's palace. But once he'd pushed his way through the hordes of slaves bustling in and out, he'd been told to go to the main entrance, the front door used by important people and guests of the royal families. The guards sneered at his humble clothing but showed him straight in.

"I have over two thousand scrolls in my collection," said the prince, indicating the high shelves on one side of the vast room. "I like to read, and to keep a record of all the facts I learn." He tapped his chest. "This heart will grow old one day and it will forget things."

"I have never seen so much knowledge gathered in one place," admitted Renni.

"We think that once something is written down, it will be preserved forever," said the prince.

"But that's not true. A lot of scrolls are lost or destroyed in floods and fires, or simply thrown away by ignorant people. I see it as my duty to protect the writings of our great nation. We are, after all, favoured by the gods above all nations, and our knowledge must be preserved for future generations. Do you agree?"

"Yes, absolutely," agreed Renni, taking another sip of milk.

"I acquire scrolls wherever I can find them," continued Prince Khaem. He leaned towards Renni and whispered, "Sometimes, I must confess, I even resort to stealing them. Or at least, I have them stolen for me. You'd be amazed how many valuable scrolls there are out there, languishing in forgotten libraries, their writing fading away simply because their greedy owners refuse to part with them. You would be surprised how thoughtless people are when it comes to scrolls. You find them in the most unlikely places. I once visited a farm where the quail coop was lined with old papyrus. The farmer had been given it in exchange for corn. I could see writing on it so I rescued it. It turned out to be an ancient poem.

"As a prince, I could order people to just give me anything I want, of course, but that would be abusing my power. Father would not be pleased." He winked at Renni, who looked shocked. "You find it scandalous, a royal prince employing common thieves?"

"No," said Renni. "I…"

"People think it must be fun being a prince, living in a palace with hundreds of slaves and servants to look after you. But the truth is, it's like living in a gilded cage. There are so many rules one must obey, so many everyday things a prince can't do that an ordinary person takes for granted. I can't suddenly decide to go out for a walk, for instance. Everything has to be planned carefully beforehand. That is why I find refuge in my scrolls. They are my escape."

Renni, who'd always thought being a prince meant you could have anything you wanted, was lost for words. Prince Khaem sounded very lonely. Perhaps that's why he was confiding in a total stranger.

"The ancients used to say that knowledge is the breath of the gods themselves," continued the prince. "By preserving it, I am helping the gods. Don't you think so?"

"Yes," mumbled Renni.

The prince indicated an enormous wooden chest at the back of the room. "My father thinks I collect myths and legends about the gods. And I do, but I also collect far more important writing. An old friend of my father's once told me that knowledge in the hands of the wrong people is very dangerous. That is why I have that chest." He smiled. "Go on, open it. I give you royal permission."

Renni walked over to the chest and tried throwing back the lid, but it seemed to be stuck.

"It's locked," grinned the prince. "No one can open it but me. You see, all the secrets inside it are safe."

He was interrupted by a slave who coughed politely from the doorway. "Your Highness," he said, "your mother, the queen Isetnofret, wishes to speak with you."

"I'm coming right away," said the prince.

He turned to Renni. "It is a pity I didn't have time to show you my sketches of Thoth inventing writing. The picture is going on the wall there, above the shelves. You must come again sometime soon. Just show my ring at the door again. I'm expecting a delivery of something very interesting that I'd like you to see."

4

An Interesting Invitation
- Renni -

"I can't believe it," said Renni. "I have a whole month with no work. Uncle Pepy said it's going to take that long for the builders to move the entrance to Pharaoh's tomb."

"What will you do for money?" asked Princess Balaal. "Will you and your family have to do without? I can help, of course."

She and Renni were lying on the roof of Renni's house, eating dates. In the distance, the swollen waters of the great river shimmered under the hot sun. They could see the tops of palm trees poking out of the flood water.

"Pharaoh has been most generous," answered

Renni. "All the artists working on the tomb will still get paid."

"It's only fair," said Princess Balaal. "After all, it was his mistake that put a stop to the work."

"Mahu is off work too," said Renni. "There's nothing to do in the fields until the flood waters recede. He tried getting some work on a building site but there's nothing going."

"I think the goddess is telling us we should have another adventure," said the princess.

"Which goddess?" asked Renni.

"Astarte," replied Balaal, "the Fenkhu goddess of power and hunting."

Renni cast his mind back to their first adventure. He thought of General Tatia and his heart scarab. Had the inscriptions on it gained him entry to the Field of Reeds?

Thoughts of the heart scarab were quickly followed by memories of Paser. What magic was the old vizier cooking up now? Was his luckless servant Abanoub still under his spell and looking for them?

Renni shuddered just thinking about the evil vizier and his powers to control people.

"I don't mean we should have an adventure like the last one," said Princess Balaal, as if reading Renni's thoughts. "I can read from your face that you don't want to face that much danger again."

"I would rather spend the time painting," admitted Renni. "But I think Mahu would welcome the excitement."

"I mean we should go exploring," said Balaal. "You know, learn things."

"What kind of things?" asked Renni.

"Before I came to the Black Land, I promised my father and my tutor that I would learn everything I can about your way of life. My father has long been fascinated by your extravagant culture."

Princess Balaal was a sort of refugee. She'd escaped from her country when her life was put in danger by people trying to steal her father's crown. She now lived with other displaced children on a small island in the middle of the great river. It was called Crocodile Island, because on it stood a forgotten temple dedicated to Sobek, the crocodile god. At the moment, the whole island was submerged under flood water and all the children who lived on it had moved to other homes. They would not return until the flood receded. Balaal was living with Renni's mother.

"So, what do you want to learn about the culture of the Black Land?"

"I find your attachment to animals fascinating," said the princess, helping herself to another date. "You seem to worship even dangerous animals like snakes and hippopotami. Your gods have animal heads."

"We respect wild animals but we also fear them," said Renni. "Crocodiles, especially, really scare me. I found your disused temple on Crocodile Island very scary. I don't know how you can sleep there."

"Yet Mahu finds crocodiles fascinating,"

remarked Balaal.

"I know," said Renni. "He even offers sacrifice to them during the harvest."

"Mahu likes danger," continued Balaal. "He's like a lot of men in my own country. They think facing danger proves that they're tough. Which is why he's already agreed to come on a journey with me. We're hoping you'll come along with us, now you have all this free time on your hands."

Renni sat up. "What journey?"

"An old friend of my father's sent me a message," said Balaal. "He's a priest in the city of Shedet."

"But that's the City of Crocodiles," gasped Renni. "It makes me shudder just to think about it."

"My father's friend tells me the crocodiles at Shedet are either tame or closely guarded by temple assistants," said Balaal. "You'll be safe. Apparently, the Great Lake outside the city is teeming with wildlife. You could draw many animals."

"We'd have to travel along the great river during the flooding season," argued Renni. "It might be dangerous."

"People travel along the swollen river all the time," said Balaal, finishing the last of the dates in the dish. "It will be fun. Even your *mut* thinks we should go."

"Mother is even more terrified of crocodiles than I am," said Renni, unconvinced.

"Mahu didn't tell her we're going to Shedet," admitted Balaal with a naughty laugh. "He just told her we're going travelling."

Mut called from the yard. "Balaal, Renni? I've taken the bread out of the oven. Do you want to come down for supper? Mahu will be home any moment."

"It's a long way to go just to practise my drawing," said Renni, picking up the empty dish. "And I'm expecting to go to the palace again in a few days."

"Who says you'll be going to Shedet just

to practise your drawing?" chuckled Balaal, a mischievous glint in her eye. "Don't you want to see a crocodile being mummified?"

5

The Ibis Again
- Mahu -

The sun was not yet up when Renni, Mahu and Balaal made their way across the city of Waset to the river. In the stillness of dawn, the calls of the birds in the reeds were shrill and insistent. Frogs croaked loudly, as if thanking Amun-Ra for a new day.

"I hope this will be a short trip," Renni yawned. "I want to be back in time to see Prince Khaem's new painting of Thoth. He said I should go back to the palace soon."

Balaal and Mahu shared a look—they had heard the prince's name pass Renni's lips many times since the boys' meeting.

"Don't worry, we won't keep you from your precious new friend too long!" Mahu teased, winking at Balaal. "Just make sure you don't lose the ring he gave you. You'll never be allowed in the palace without it and he'll think you've run off with it."

Renni gulped and checked his bag to make sure the ring was safe.

Mahu chuckled, then stopped on the swollen bank of the river. "Look, our ship awaits!" He pointed to a vessel tied to a palm tree poking out of the water.

"It's beautiful," gasped Renni. "I like the bright colours. It's like a waterborne rainbow."

"You've done a magnificent job repairing it, Mahu," said Balaal, impressed. "I'm glad I bought it. Are you sure you don't want to be a carpenter rather than a sailor?"

Mahu shook his head and grinned from ear to ear as he looked at the boat. This wasn't the grand vessel of his dreams. It wasn't big enough to have a proper crew or go on the big, wide sea. But it was a step in the right direction. It was made of solid wood rather than papyrus reeds like his skiff, and it had a linen mast which he'd darned and patched. There was even a little cabin for when the sun got too fierce.

"Come on," he said. "Let's get aboard."

"Wait," said Princess Balaal. "In my country, we believe in Yam, the powerful god of the sea and rivers. We must offer him sacrifice so he will protect us from danger."

She pulled a charm off the silver chain around her neck and threw it in the water. "May Yam protect this little ship and all who sail in her."

The three waded deeper into the water and clambered aboard, Mahu going first to establish his role as captain. Renni carried a basket of food and milk *Mut* had given them.

Using the oars, they pushed away from the tree and headed into the middle of the river. Soon there was a fair wind that filled the sail, which had the eye of Horus painted on it for good luck.

The sun came up in a glorious blaze of light, turning the river into molten gold.

"Look, Amun-Ra has awoken," said Renni. "May his passage across the sky today shine on us all."

Mahu had been told that the river journey to the city of Shedet would take only a few days, especially if there was wind in their sail. The city stood in an oasis on the banks of the Great Lake Balaal had mentioned to Renni. It was the most ancient city of the Black Land.

The journey was pleasant, with much to see on the riverbank. The children passed a village where the flood had reached almost to the tops of the houses. Entire families were camping on the flat roofs, roasting fish on open fires. It sounded, from the loud singing and laughter, like they were having a wonderful time.

Further along the river, they came across a family of hippos sprawled out on a large rock. The mother had a new calf and she bellowed fiercely as the boat sailed past, warning the children to keep away.

They soon ate up all the food *Mut* had given them, so they fished in the river. To Mahu's astonishment, the fish seemed to leap into his net. *Perhaps the current in the flood water has made them reckless*, Mahu thought. *Or perhaps someone on the other side is looking after us.* After the adventure of the heart scarab, Mahu had started to take the gods a little more seriously.

On the third night, they tied their boat to a large tree with overhanging branches. Tired of the usual fish, Mahu hunted around in the muddy bank and caught some crabs. They roasted them over a fire, then huddled on the boat to enjoy them. It was a chilly night.

Mahu was relishing the last of the crab when something dropped out of the branches overhead and snatched it right out his hands.

"Ouch!" he cried. "That nearly got my fingers."

"It's just an ibis," laughed Renni. "The poor

thing must be hungry." He held out his last bit of food. "Here, son of Thoth. Have some more."

Mahu glared angrily at the river bird which was clacking its curved beak as it devoured Renni's offering. He'd been enjoying the last of his dinner.

"Shoo," he said, waving his arms at the bird. "You got what you wanted, now go away."

"Don't insult him," warned Balaal. "Something feels different about this ibis."

"What do you mean?" asked Renni.

"It's just a feeling," replied Balaal. "I get goosebumps when there's magic nearby." She held up her arm. "I have them now, look."

Mahu glared at the ibis. Once again, he had the distinct impression that he was looking into a human eye. But, once more, the sensation lasted only a moment. Mahu shook his head to clear it.

"Magic or not, that bird seems to have taken a shine to you," said Renni. "Maybe it's trying to protect you from something."

"I don't need protecting," growled Mahu, secretly feeling nervous about something he couldn't fully explain. "I can take care of myself and, as captain of this boat, I can take care of you too."

He threw a stick at the ibis. It took off with a loud grunt, but soon returned and settled on the deck.

Balaal held out her hand, muttering under her breath. The ibis looked at her curiously and answered with a throaty murmuring sound of its own. Mahu watched in amazement as the wild bird waddled over to the princess and let her stroke the top of its head.

6

A Cart in the Night
- Renni -

Amun-Ra's solar boat had sailed across the sky once more before they reached a small port outside a busy settlement with low, mud-brick walls.

"The actual port is underwater at this time of year," called a farmer who was about to cross the river in a skiff piled dangerously high with vegetables. "Are you on a pilgrimage to one of our famous crocodile temples?"

"*One* of your famous crocodile temples?" repeated Renni.

The farmer opened his arms wide. "You are in the Land of the Lakes, my friend. One of the most important regions of the Black Land. We have many settlements here dedicated to the great god Sobek."

"We are going to the temple in Shedet," said Balaal.

"Ah, the oldest city of all," said the farmer. "I believe there is going to be a special wrapping ceremony tomorrow. The Golden One is dead. Not that ordinary children would be allowed to watch the ceremony, of course. Many would like to go but few are ever invited."

The three children smiled at each other. Was this the crocodile they had come to see being mummified?

"Who is the Golden One?" asked Renni.

"The sacred crocodile that lived in the temple pond," explained the farmer. "We call him the Golden One because he is festooned with golden necklaces and pendants given to him by wealthy visitors. The priests tamed him so well, he used to eat fried fish and honey cakes straight from their hands. It's true, I'm telling you. I saw it with my own eyes once when I was delivering vegetables to the temple."

"And what will happen now the Golden One is dead?" asked Balaal.

"The priests of Sobek will choose a new one," replied the farmer. "If you stay long enough in the city, you might see the choosing ceremony yourselves. It takes place outdoors so anyone can watch."

He nodded at the baskets on his boat. "I wish I could attend myself but sadly I have work to do. Anyway, the best way to get to Shedet is by staying in your boat. There's a canal further up the bank which connects the sacred river to the Great Lake. Once there, you can walk to the city. Good luck, and say a prayer to Sobek for me. I live in fear of crocodiles. They're not all as tame as the Golden One."

Bidding the farmer goodbye, the children sailed on, the wind filling their sail. The ibis followed them, often perching on the mast or wheeling high up in the air.

They soon came to the canal and followed other boats away from the main river. The sun set and a bright moon rose, illuminating the land around them. They sailed through rocky desert for a while, but it soon gave way to green land again.

By sunrise, they had reached the Great Lake and docked at a busy jetty.

While Renni and Mahu tied the boat, Balaal paid a local girl to keep an eye on it. "We'll be gone a few days at the most. Look after it well," she said, giving the girl a silver bracelet. "There'll be another one when we get back."

Renni looked around him as Mahu made sure the boat was tied securely. Balaal had been right about the wildlife on the lake. There seemed to be water birds roosting in every clump of reeds. Renni wished he had time to stop and draw a few sketches on his tablet but Mahu nudged him forwards.

"Hurry up, little brother."

They didn't need to ask directions to the city; they could see its walls rising high out of the flat land ahead. Renni reckoned they'd reach it in no time, but it seemed that their eyes were deceiving them. By late afternoon, the city was still quite far off.

"We should find shelter for the night," said Mahu. "City gates are always closed at sundown. I don't know about you two, but I don't want to be outside when it gets dark. It'll be freezing."

They found a stone hut that smelt strongly of goat droppings—a shelter used by shepherds and goatherds. Renni led the way in, holding his nose against the powerful stench. After a quick supper of figs, they all stretched out on a pile of damp straw—Renni suspected, with disgust, that goats had weed in it. Mahu and Balaal were soon fast asleep, the princess's hand resting on the hilt of her curved sword.

Renni remained awake. It was eerily silent

except for the moaning of the wind outside the hut. He prayed to the gods for protection. It was said that the wind was really the crying of lost *ka*s, looking for a body to inhabit.

He heard a familiar sound outside. It was their old friend the ibis, muttering loudly. Renni watched in astonishment as the bird flapped into the hut. It made straight for Mahu and poked him in the foot with its beak.

Mahu grunted in his sleep but did not wake up. The ibis turned its beady eye on Renni.

Renni felt the hairs on the back of his neck rise. The ibis seemed to have human eyes. Or was he dreaming? He shook his head. No—he was definitely awake. He'd only been imagining things. Looking again, the ibis had the eyes of a bird. It was staring at him and clucking repeatedly. Was it *beckoning* to him? Renni got to his feet. The ibis soared through the doorway and he followed it.

Outside, a bent figure was pulling a cart along

the road. It wasn't an ordinary wooden cart, the kind Renni saw every day on the streets in Waset. It seemed to be cobbled together from bits of broken chariot. An enormous box was perched on top of it, tied securely with rope. In the moonlight, it looked very much like a sarcophagus.

The boy pulling it was singing above the sound of the wind. His head wrapped in a shawl and his face hidden, he seemed to be lost in a world of his own. Renni was about to call out, to ask the boy if he wanted to stop for a rest, when the ibis fluttered against his face, knocking him back.

By the time a stunned Renni got back up on his feet, the strange cart had disappeared round a bend and the sound of the boy's singing was growing fainter. The ibis settled on the branch of a nearby tree.

Renni stared at it. Balaal was right. There was something special about that bird, something he couldn't explain. It wasn't just following them because they were feeding it or because it had adopted Mahu.

Perhaps it was protecting them. Renni was sure it had wanted Mahu to see the boy with the cart and, failing to wake him, had made sure Renni would see it instead.

But why? Who was that boy pulling the strange cart? What was in the strange box he was dragging all the way to Shedet?

Feeding the Sacred Crocodiles
- Mahu -

They reached the city at dawn, just as the gates were being opened. A river of people swarmed around them: pilgrims come to visit the temples, children selling food, and soldiers, still in uniform, returning home on leave. Shedet was almost as busy as Waset, Mahu thought.

Balaal asked the way to the temple and a woman with a large basket of fruit on her head pointed them in the right direction.

"We are looking for a priest called Yuyu," said Balaal as they entered the temple through a gate decorated with crocodile teeth.

"What does he look like?" asked Renni.

"I'm not sure," said Balaal. "I haven't seen him since I was a baby."

"You'll recognise him without a problem then," laughed Mahu.

"But I will," said Balaal confidently. "And he will recognise me. We of the Fenkhu are bound together in spirit."

A priest hurried over, a wide smile on his face. He was a short man, with muscular shoulders. His dark eyes were tiny but they sparkled like polished gem stones. "Your Highness, welcome," he said, joining his hands and bowing. "I was looking out for you."

"Very pleased to see you, Uncle Yuyu," said Balaal. "May the gods of the Fenkhu bless your every step." She turned to Mahu and Renni. "Yuyu's not really my uncle. It's just a term we use back home when greeting very close friends."

Yuyu bowed to Balaal. "I've known this girl since she was a baby in the royal cot. I was her special guardian, tasked with offering prayers to

protect her every hour of the day. If I remember right, she loved having her tiny feet tickled."

"Yes, and Father used to say I'd bawl my head off every time you came near my cot," teased Balaal. "I must have thought you were a monster."

The priest chuckled at her joke. "Are you not going to introduce me to your friends?"

"This is Mahu," said the princess. "He is a sailor in the making."

The priest joined his hands on his chest by way of greeting. "A noble calling, the sea. May Yam and Sobek, the gods of water, protect you on your voyages."

"And this is Renni, his younger brother," said Balaal. "He is an artist."

"I'm only a *sesh qedut*, an apprentice," said Renni humbly.

"He is working on Pharaoh's tomb," added Balaal, "Pharaoh himself has praised his work."

"Well done and welcome," said the priest. "As an artist, you will find much to look at in the Great

Temple of Sobek. Though my father is from the land of the Fenkhu, my mother was from the Black Land and I am a priest of Sobek." He swept an arm grandly around the vast enclosure which was surrounded by a high mudbrick wall. "Impressive, isn't it? There are a lot of temples dedicated to the crocodile god, even here in the Land of the Lakes, but this is by far the greatest. I sincerely believe that Sobek himself resides in this temple, unseen by the human eye but present nevertheless. We call him *Sobek Shedety*, protector of the city."

Mahu looked around him. The complex was huge. Right in front of him was the main temple with highly polished steps leading up to a wide entrance between tall pillars. To his right was a long, low building with open doorways and next to it, a grander one with proper doors.

"The lower building houses the guest quarters," said Yuyu. "You will be staying there. The one further along is where the priests live. It looks grand from the outside but it's quite humble inside. There are other buildings at the far end of the enclosure; shrines to Hathor, Amun-Ra and Knut. And of course, we have our special cages where the crocodiles are kept—and our famous sacred pond. Come, I'll show you."

The three children followed Yuyu across the enclosure, its dusty floor shimmering in the intense heat. A crowd was gathered by the pond, shouting excitedly.

"Ah, they are waiting for the daily ceremony," said Yuyu. "It is feeding time."

The pond was vast with a tiled floor, its water reflecting the deep blue of the sky. An enormous statue of Sobek rearing up on his hind legs stood behind it, water gushing out from between his pointed teeth.

Mahu stared, fascinated, as a young priest dived into the pool and pulled back the bolt on a small door underwater. By the time his companions had pulled him out again, a glistening snout had pushed the door open. One small crocodile after another rose to the surface of the water, their eyes fixed hungrily on the audience around the pool.

Mahu admired crocodiles. He was in awe of their strength and power and wished he had their sense of cunning when hunting or fishing. But there was something even more alluring about these young crocodiles, something… mesmerising. Perhaps they really were touched by the gods.

"There are seven of them," explained Yuyu. "A magic number. They are the offspring of the Golden One, who was himself one of seven hatchlings."

"Ah, the Golden One," said Balaal. "We've heard all about him."

Yuyu nodded sadly. "The gods, in their infinite wisdom, called him to the Field of Reeds. We have embalmed his body in a process that took seventy days. Tonight is the final wrapping ceremony—the one I invited you to watch—which is when we put him in the sarcophagus. Tomorrow, one of these young crocodiles will be chosen as his successor."

There was a clashing of cymbals and a procession of priests filed out of the main temple. Each one of them carried a dish piled high with fried fish.

An older priest clad in crocodile skin followed them, singing loudly.

"That is Pareneffer," said Yuyu. "As the high priest of Sobek, he is one of the most powerful people in the Black Land. It is said he advises Pharaoh on matters of faith and celebration. The others are junior priests but they too will be important people one day. They will serve in some of the most famous temples in our country."

Pareneffer stopped by the pool and, calling on Sobek to witness the sacrifice, nodded at the young priests who stepped forward and emptied the dishes into the pool. Immediately, the water turned to white foam as the hungry crocodiles leapt and fought for the food. Mahu watched, rapt with attention, until all the offerings had been devoured and the crocodiles sank to the bottom of the pool. He'd never seen anything so dangerous... and exciting.

"Now, all you worshippers of Sobek, come forward and offer your own sacrifice," called

Pareneffer. The crowd surged forward and started throwing honey cakes into the water.

"Please," scolded Yuyu gently, "do it with respect. This is an act of worship, not entertainment."

The crocodiles leapt back to the surface with incredible speed, some breaking clean out of the water, their jaws snapping wildly.

"My hand! My hand!" screamed a worshipper. "The crocodile got my hand!"

8

The Final Wrapping
- Mahu -

Mahu felt the blood drain from his face and he quickly pulled his brother back from the edge of the pool. "Renni, don't look. Let's get away from here."

It was too late. Renni was staring in horror at the injured man. Balaal slipped an arm round his waist. "Are you alright? You're not going to faint, are you?"

"I'll be fine," mumbled Renni, his voice catching in his throat. "Just a bit shook up, that's all. Let's get away."

"Good idea," said Yuyu. "We always warn people to be careful when feeding the crocodiles. There is a good side to Sobek, but he can also be cruel."

He led the way round the main temple to the long building where the guests lodged. "I have had a room prepared for you boys and a separate chamber for Her Highness."

"Any room good enough for my friends is good enough for me," insisted Balaal.

Yuyu frowned. "But, Your Highness, it is perhaps not fit for a princess to share quarters with commoners."

"Yuyu," snapped Balaal. "I said I shall stay in the same room as my friends."

The priest bowed. "As you wish, Your Highness."

He opened the door to a room, which was simply furnished with cots, a reed mat on the floor and a jug of water on a low table. "There is fruit and bread if you get hungry. I'll see you tonight for the wrapping ceremony. There will be a crowd there too, but it will be different from the lot around the pool. Only people with the right connections get invited to wrapping ceremonies."

As Yuyu left, Renni slumped down on one of the cots. He was still shaking. Mahu brought him some water from the jug.

"Here, little brother, drink up."

"I love and honour the gods," said Renni, taking the cup. "But I have to admit, I don't think Sobek is a god I'd choose to worship."

"Just rest now," said Mahu gently. "You'll feel much better after a nap. I'll wake you when it's time for the ceremony."

The ceremony started in the dead of night. A crowd of invited onlookers was gathered in the mortuary room behind the Great Temple. The air was thick with incense, making Mahu's throat dry. He coughed into his hand and threw a sideways glance at his brother. Renni had stopped shaking and was looking around with keen interest. Balaal was smiling. She was looking forward to the ceremony.

Mahu was looking forward to it too, but not for the same reason as Renni and Balaal. While they saw this as a holy ritual, he thought of it more as a piece of entertainment, featuring a crocodile.

Since the adventure of the heart scarab, Mahu had begun to believe more in the power of the gods. But there was still a part of him that rebelled against the idea. He almost wished that the gods didn't exist, that people could live free of the fear that their *ka* might one day be gobbled up by Ammut.

A door opened and the dead crocodile was carried in on a litter. Mahu was amazed by the Golden One's sheer size and powerful tail, still lethal-looking even though it was thickly wrapped in cloth.

At the head of the procession walked Pareneffer, holding a tray with four jars. They all had carved heads on the lids. Mahu knew what was inside them: the vital organs from the crocodile's body. A priest in a black hood walked behind the mummy.

He carried a was-sceptre, a long walking stick topped with the head of a strange animal. Not a real animal, Mahu knew, but a symbol of the god Set. People called it the Set-animal.

The priests placed the carcass on a marble table. Through the haze of incense, Mahu, Renni and Balaal watched Pareneffer tuck spells written on strips of papyrus and amulets between the layers of cloth. The other priests wound a final layer of fine linen around the crocodile's body. The mummy was complete.

Pareneffer and the priests stepped away, leaving only one near the table. He still had his cowl over his face. Only his chin was visible as he opened a small wooden chest and held up a golden mask shaped like a crocodile's face and snout. He placed it on the crocodile.

"Behold, a gift for the dear departed Golden One from the priests of Sobek."

Mahu's blood ran cold at the sound of that voice. It was Paser, the evil vizier.

9

A Difficult Decision

- Renni -

"What is *he* doing here?" said Balaal. "I thought he was ill and unable to leave his mansion."

She, Renni and Mahu had returned to the guest room, all three of them stunned by what they'd just seen and heard.

"No doubt he lied to Pharaoh," said Mahu.

"But isn't he afraid people might recognise him?" wondered Renni.

"I don't suppose many people who know him in Waset travel this far," said Mahu. "There are closer Sobek temples."

"Still," said Renni, "he's running a risk."

"Which can only mean one thing," said Balaal.

"He's in Shedet to do something really important, something worth taking a risk for."

"Balaal is right," Mahu cut in. "The vizier wouldn't risk travelling all the way here just to help mummify a crocodile, even if it is the Golden One. There's got to be something more to his visit than that."

"Let's find out what he's up to," said Balaal.

Renni looked from her to Mahu. "Why? It's got nothing to do with us. The last time we locked horns with the vizier, we put ourselves in great danger. I don't want to do it again."

"I don't trust that man," said Mahu. "I'm sure he's up to no good. And his plotting might involve us. After all, we did ruin his plans before. Perhaps he wants to pay us back."

Renni felt a tightening in his stomach. Coming to the Land of the Lakes had turned out to be a huge mistake. First, there was that business with the hungry crocodile at the sacred pool, and now Mahu and Balaal were wanting to poke their noses into a dangerous man's affairs.

I'm just an artist, thought Renni. *All I want is to paint pictures in temples and tombs.*

And then he thought back to when he had returned the heart scarab to General Tatia's tomb. He remembered the sight of the god Anubis waiting with the scales of justice in the stars.

Would his heart weigh lighter than Ma'at's feather if he refused to help Mahu and Balaal? Would the god-judges hold his cowardice against him?

"Alright," he said reluctantly. "Let's try and find out what the vizier is really doing here. But we have to pray to Ma'at first. She will keep us safe."

10

The Sacred Pool

- Renni -

"How are we going to find out why Paser is in Shedet?" asked Balaal.

"We'll have to shadow him," said Mahu. "And we should start right away. Come on, let's get going."

They let themselves out, tiptoeing past the other guest rooms. They were not the only ones wandering around in the dead of night. Someone was approaching a drinking fountain. It was the boy Renni had seen dragging the sarcophagus past the shepherd's hut. He threw back his cowl and put his lips to the waterspout.

"Isn't that… Abanoub?" gasped Renni.

"It is," hissed back Balaal. "He must have come here with the vizier. I'll see what he's up to."

"Good idea," said Mahu. "Renni and I will search for the vizier. We'll meet up on the steps of the main temple."

His heart beating fast in his chest, Renni followed Mahu to the priests' quarters. They tried the front door but there wasn't even a handle. You could only get into the building by knocking to alert a servant. They tried the goods entrance round the back, but that was firmly shut too. Mahu checked the windows; they were too small to squeeze through, even for Renni.

"What do we do now?" Renni asked.

"I'll try and climb onto the roof," said Mahu. "There might be a part of the building that's topped only with papyrus reeds."

He was about to look for a foothold when Renni stopped him. "Listen. Did you hear that grunt? The ibis is here."

The bird was indeed perched on top of the building. With another grunt, it took off and glided towards the other end of the house.

"I think it might be showing us a way in," said Renni. He and Mahu followed it. The ibis settled on top of a clay bread oven in an outdoor kitchen. It scratched at it with its claws, muttering under its breath.

"I think that silly bird is just begging for food," said Mahu.

"You're wrong," Renni whispered back. "I know

what it's telling us. I've worked with Uncle Pepy in grand houses that have ovens like this. Help me push it aside."

Putting their shoulders against the rough clay, the two of them managed to move the oven, revealing a large hole in the mud brick wall.

"It's so the heat from the oven can keep this part of the building warm," explained Renni. "It's also a way in."

"Good thinking, little brother," said Mahu. "Come on, let's go."

He ducked into the tunnel and Renni crawled in after him. They came out in a storeroom, piled high with sacks and storage jars. Mahu tried the door and it opened.

Renni looked over his brother's shoulder. A large dog was fast asleep just outside the door, snoring loudly. Mahu urged his brother forward. Clutching his sidelock amulet for luck, Renni stepped carefully over the sleeping dog and tiptoed after his brother. Turning a corner, they found themselves in a large dining room. Plates and beer jugs were laid out on the table for the morning meal. A statue of Sobek stood at one end, a lamp burning in front of it.

The boys hurried out into a corridor lined with doors on either side. One of them was ajar. Someone in the room was arguing.

"Yes, Paser, but do we have to do it now? It's been a very long day."

It was Pareneffer, the chief priest. Renni froze.

"Never forget I made you what you are today, cousin," he heard Paser say.

Cousin? Renni turned to Mahu, his eyes wide with shock. The vizier and Pareneffer were *cousins?*

"And I can have you replaced in an instant," continued the vizier. "All it would take is a word in Pharaoh's ear."

"Very well," said Pareneffer, sounding defeated. "Let's get it over and done with then."

Renni and Mahu barely had time to step away from the door before Paser and Pareneffer came out. They ducked back into the dark as the two men turned in the opposite direction and walked on, Paser carrying his was-sceptre. Renni breathed a sigh of relief. The gods were on their side. They hadn't been spotted.

The front door opened and closed again. Renni and Mahu waited a few moments, then peered round a corner to see if there was still a servant on night door duty. No one was about. Renni opened the door and they slipped through.

Paser and Pareneffer were hurrying up the steps to the main temple. The chief priest unlocked the door and he and Paser disappeared inside.

Renni and Mahu hurried after them. Renni tried

the door but, just as he'd expected, Pareneffer had locked it behind him. Suddenly an arm reached out and pulled him behind a pillar. Renni nearly screamed.

"Sssh! It's only me: Balaal."

"Paser and Pareneffer are in there," gasped Renni, sighing with relief.

"I know," said Balaal. "I saw them going in."

"Did you manage to find out what Abanoub is up to?" asked Mahu.

Balaal frowned. "No, he seems to have vanished."

"We need to get in the temple as quickly as we can," said Mahu.

"But the door is locked," Renni added.

Balaal smiled. "As the priests of our beloved Yam like to say, if you can't reach the sky, try the water."

She closed her eyes and started humming softly.

"What is she doing?" Mahu whispered to Renni.

Balaal opened one eye. "I am communing

with Yam. Asking for help. Now please, let me concentrate. We haven't much time."

She continued humming and the wind rose, tousling her hair. An owl hooted in the distance. When Balaal opened her eyes again, she was smiling.

"My hunch was right. Yam has shown me a way in. Come with me."

She led the way to the pool where the ibis was flapping away happily. "Can you two hold your breath underwater?"

"Of course," said Mahu. "All the kids who live near the Great River can."

"Mahu's right," said Renni. "But I'm not going in that pool. I'm not swimming with crocodiles."

"The crocodiles have obviously been moved to an indoor pond for the night," Balaal assured him. "Otherwise they would have attacked the ibis."

"But what has this pond got to do with the temple?" asked Mahu.

"It's very much like the temple of Yam back

home," replied Balaal. "That has a sacred pond too, except we don't keep crocodiles in it, we have freshwater fish. And that underwater gate the priests opened to let the crocodiles out for the feeding ceremony? I'll bet my sword that the canal behind it is connected to a reservoir under the temple. It would be the main source of water for the whole complex. That way, if the temple ever gets attacked and the whole community has to lock itself in, it will always have access to water."

"You mean we can *swim* into the temple?" said Mahu.

Balaal nodded. "Yam willing."

"Then wait for me here," said Mahu, handing Renni his tunic. "I'll see if Balaal's right."

Renni hardly dared to watch as Mahu dived into the pool. He half-expected to hear the splash of crocodiles leaping but there was only the sound of Balaal whispering, "Yam go with you."

"And Sobek," muttered Renni.

He could dimly see Mahu open the tunnel door and disappear inside. Tense moments passed and no crocodiles emerged. Neither did Mahu.

"Something's happened to him," Renni panicked. "The crocodiles must have got him."

"They haven't," said Balaal. "Look."

Renni peered into the water again. He saw someone floating up towards them. "Come on," said Mahu, breaking the surface. "There *is* a way in."

Relieved to see his brother safe and sound, Renni took off his tunic and tucked it with Mahu's behind a statue of Sobek. He jumped gingerly into the pool, expecting the water to be as cold as the Great River. But it was surprisingly warm. Watching Balaal through screwed up eyes, he followed her into the tunnel.

It was suffocatingly narrow and pitch dark. Renni fought the panic rising in his chest. He knew he had to keep calm or he would drown.

Renni shivered and kicked harder with his feet, propelling himself forward. After what felt like an eternity, he shot out into wide, open water. He'd reached the underground cistern. A few more moments later, he was gasping for breath at the surface. Soft green light was glowing far above.

"Beautiful, isn't it?" said Balaal, who had already surfaced close by. "It's made by thousands of tiny creatures. Their tails glow in the dark."

"It's like looking up at the stars," said Renni.

"Very pretty, I'm sure," said Mahu, "but let's get up to the temple."

Clambering out of the cistern, they found themselves in a vast hall paved with enormous smooth slabs. Square columns decorated with images of Sobek were holding up the ceiling.

"There's a door there, look," said Mahu.

It opened onto a flight of narrow, wet, slippery stairs. They went up them carefully. At the top was a second door, which creaked a little as they opened it.

The room beyond it was lit by lamps set on narrow tables. Rows of wooden shelves lined the walls, rising right up to the ceiling. Renni stared in horror.

The shelves were all packed with mummified crocodiles.

The Crocodile Mummy
- Renni -

Renni's skin started to crawl. The crocodiles had their eyes covered with patches of cloth but they still seemed to be looking directly at him.

"These crocodiles must have belonged to very important people," said Mahu. "Look, some of the mummies are decorated with sacred symbols and patterns."

"And jewellery," said Balaal. "But where are the sarcophagi?"

"Not all animal mummies have them," said Renni. "I helped Uncle Pepy paint a funeral scene once and the animals in it didn't have coffins." He looked round. "This is going to give me nightmares."

"Let's find the way out then," said Mahu.

But just then, they heard voices. Balaal quickly shut the door and Mahu pulled Renni down under a table. Balaal joined them.

Renni recognised the approaching voices at once. They were Paser and Pareneffer.

"Do you know which one it is you want?" said Pareneffer, stepping through a door at the other end of the room.

"Yes," snapped the vizier. "It is painted all over with cobras. It shouldn't be hard to spot." He grabbed a torch and started looking along the shelves.

"A cobra pattern," said Pareneffer slowly, following Paser. "A very unusual choice for a mummy, I'm sure you'll agree…"

Paser turned suddenly. "I know from my… research—"

"Research?" laughed Pareneffer nervously. "You mean you were informed by your *spies*. I know you have spies everywhere, cousin."

"…that there are exactly ninety-seven crocodiles in here," continued Paser, ignoring the insult. "And just in case Pharaoh suddenly takes it into his head to count how many mummies he has in all his temples—he's been known to do sudden audits like that, as His Majesty considers all the animal mummies in the Black Land as his by divine right—I have taken the necessary precautions."

He called out. "Get in here, boy."

There was the sound of something coming *bump, bump, bump* down the stairs. Someone appeared at the open door, dragging a sarcophagus. It was Abanoub!

Renni thought of the poor boy pulling the heavy cart all the way from the lake to Shedet. How had he managed to do it? Perhaps the vizier had put a spell on him, to give him the strength.

"My trusted minion has brought a replacement," chuckled the vizier. He opened the sarcophagus and lifted out a crocodile mummy. "See, I've

had one of the best artists in the country decorate it with a similar cobra pattern." He winked at Pareneffer, waving his was-sceptre. "An artist who does not even *remember* the little favour he did for me, if you know what I mean."

"Sadly, I do know what you mean," replied Pareneffer. "You seem to have gone to a lot of trouble. What is so important about this mummy you want?"

Paser put a finger to his lips. "The less you know, the better, cousin. Now let's get on with the search."

The two men started walking along the shelves. Renni hoped they wouldn't notice the wet footprints the children had left on the floor. He held his breath.

"Strange, it doesn't seem to be here," snarled Paser, walking right past the children's hiding place.

"But there are exactly ninety-seven mummies in the room, just as you said," said Pareneffer.

"I've counted."

"Yes," growled Paser, marching across the room to a shelf. "But this mummy here just doesn't look right… It seems to have been made by an amateur! It's as fake as the one I brought."

He ripped the mummy off the shelf and tore the bandages away with his bare hands. "See, there's no crocodile in it. It's stuffed with blank papyrus."

He hurled the mummy to the floor.

"Paser… control yourself," mumbled the chief priest.

The vizier put up a hand to stop him. "But what have we here?" he said, picking a scrap of linen from the shelf with the forked end of the was-sceptre. He held it to the light. "You can make out the head of a cobra on this, do you see? The mummy I want *was* here but someone switched it with the fake one. In a hurry, I would say. The real mummy caught on a nail and this bit tore off."

"I assure you…" began Pareneffer.

Paser's eyes narrowed with suppressed rage.

He held up the was-sceptre. In the corner of the room, Abanoub whimpered.

"Quiet, boy," hissed Paser. "I have heard enough lies. I want the truth and I shall have it." He smiled as the eyes on the Set-animal started to glow a bright red. "Look into its eyes, Pareneffer. Look deep, I command you."

"I refuse," said Pareneffer. "It is forbidden to use magic on a priest."

"But the Set-animal controls everything," replied Paser, bringing the was-sceptre closer to Pareneffer. "It is impossible to disobey my order while I hold it. It gives me power over you. Look deeper into the eyes and tell me the truth. *The power of Set commands you.*"

Unable to resist, Pareneffer's eyes stared into the Set-animal's. His own turned glassy. Paser chuckled deep in his throat. "Now, cousin, you are under my spell. You have no choice but to tell me the truth. There is only one way someone can have got in here and out again with a mummy.

You must have let them in. *You* must have sold it to them. Well, did you?"

Pareneffer's voice was barely a whisper as he replied. "I—I did."

"And who did you sell the mummy to?" asked Paser calmly.

"The buyer…. didn't come here himself," replied Pareneffer. "I only dealt with his slaves. They arrived some days ago. They had a document with his royal seal to prove who had sent them. I didn't dare refuse them."

"A royal seal?" said Paser icily. "Then who sent them?"

Pareneffer hesitated a moment before replying. "His Highness, Prince Khaemwaset."

12

The Mummy's Secret
- Mahu -

Paser was silent for a long moment. Mahu could hear his breathing coming in short, angry gasps. "Well, who would have thought it? That spoilt little brat of a prince!"

He turned to Abanoub, who was still cowering in the corner. "Boy, wake up my chariot driver. We need to get to my boat on the lake at once. The prince's slaves may still be on their way to Waset. We must intercept them before the mummy reaches the palace."

He thumped the floor angrily with the was-sceptre, making Mahu flinch. "Hurry up, if the prince dabbles with what's inside that mummy, he will die. Not that I care about that, of course. But the thing can only be used once. Go on, boy, do as I say."

"Yes, master," Abanoub muttered flatly. He shuffled up the stairs, leaving the fake mummy on the floor. Paser clicked his fingers at Pareneffer to bring him out of the was-sceptre's spell. "And you, *cousin*, stay out of my way."

He strode out of the room and Pareneffer followed stiffly. The door slammed shut behind them.

"Well, I guess we found out what the vizier came to Shedet for," Mahu said, crawling out of his hiding place. He felt stiff after being cramped under the table.

"A crocodile mummy," said Balaal.

"With something dangerous inside it that could kill Prince Khaem," continued Renni. "I hate to think what it could be."

13

Isis and Neferu

- Renni -

"What could be inside the mummy that's so dangerous?" wondered Balaal.

"Whatever it is, Prince Khaem can't want it for the same reason as Paser," said Renni. "Paser is evil. The prince is good."

Balaal made a face. "In my experience, no one, not even royalty, is totally good. That's something only you people of the Black Land believe. You're obsessed with royalty."

"But Prince Khaem is a good person, as well as being half-god," insisted Renni. "He did say he was expecting a delivery of something exciting. Perhaps he meant the crocodile mummy." He looked from Balaal to Mahu. "We've got to warn him that his life is in danger."

"But surely," said Balaal, "a prince is trained to look after himself?"

"Prince Khaem is different," argued Renni. "He doesn't think like his brothers. He's not a general in the making."

"Renni is right," said Mahu. "It's our duty to warn him. We need to get to Waset as soon as possible. Let's get back to our boat."

They went up the stairs carefully, which led to the grand embalming room. The air was still heavy with the smell of incense from the ceremony, but thankfully, there was no one about.

A second door led them into the priests' dressing chamber. Robes hung from hooks on the walls. Sacred objects used in ceremonies were laid out on a long table.

Mahu peeped through a curtain. Behind it was the temple's main hall. This was not deserted. Temple assistants were lighting lamps for the first ceremony of the day. Others were busy sweeping the floor with short rush brushes. Two women in flowing robes were decking the statue of Sobek with flowers. Outside, there was the murmur of a waiting crowd.

"How will we get past them without being seen?" asked Renni, having a peep himself.

"We just wait until the crowd outside is let in," replied Mahu. "It'll be easy to slip out."

The front door opened and Pareneffer hurried in.

"Is everything ready? It's nearly sunrise," he snapped at the temple assistants. He was obviously in a bad mood. Renni wondered if he remembered anything that had happened in the crypt.

"We're late with the first sacrifice of the day," growled Pareneffer. "There's a large crowd outside waiting to witness the choosing of the new Golden One. Put those brooms away. I'll get my robe."

"He's coming this way," gasped Renni.

"Quick, get back to the preparation room,"

hissed Balaal. Just then the temple door opened again and Yuyu came in. Swooping in above him was a bird, grunting loudly.

The ibis!

Hearing the sound, Pareneffer turned on his heels. "Yuyu, what in the name of the gods…? Get that scruffy bird out of here. It is desecrating the temple."

Yuyu glanced at the ibis, which perched on a statue of Sobek, with what seemed like amusement. "It seems to be at home to me. Perhaps it is Thoth himself visiting his old friend."

Pareneffer shook his head angrily and grabbed a broom from a temple assistant. "Nonsense. That bird's not magnificent enough to be a god in disguise. I'll get rid of it."

As Pareneffer flailed the broom about, the ibis fluttered back towards the front door. Yuyu opened it to let it out and the crowd, tired of waiting, surged in.

"Get back! We are not ready yet," shouted

Pareneffer. But no one was listening. Within moments, the temple was teeming with enthusiastic pilgrims, chanting and strewing flowers.

"That bird's come to our rescue," said Mahu. "Now's our chance. Go."

The three of them slipped through the crowd, out into the morning sunshine. The ibis fluttered above them, waving its wings triumphantly. It soared high up into the air.

Renni caught sight of Abanoub at the other end of the enclosure. He was talking to a chariot driver, who was replacing a wheel.

"That must be Paser's chariot," Renni pointed.

"Great! It looks like we have a head start on the vizier," chuckled Balaal. "Let's find someone to take us back to the lake. It'll save time."

They hurried along the busy streets of Shedet until they came to the marketplace. Asking around, they found a fish trader returning to the Great Lake on her donkey cart.

"Can we hitch a ride?" asked Mahu. "We'll pay, of course."

"I'll give her one of the charms from my necklace," said Balaal.

"I might have something," said Renni, rifling through his bag. "You're always paying for us." He rummaged around, making sure as always that the prince's ring was still safely in there. It was much too precious to trade, of course, and he might never be able to get in to see Prince

Khaem without it. He found two paint brushes, their bristles were frayed but clean.

"My brother will love these," said the girl. She gestured towards the cart which was decorated with pictures of fish. "He painted all of these. My name's Isis, by the way, after the goddess. The donkey's called Neferu. She's my best friend. Hop on, everyone. And mind the oil jar. It cost me ten baskets of fish."

Mahu, Renni and Balaal clambered aboard, trying not to mind the fishy smell. Isis called out to Neferu and the donkey started trotting. "Faster, faster," she urged. Neferu eagerly picked up speed, breaking into a canter, so that the wagon bounced and careened through the busy streets.

"You seem to be in a hurry, friend," cried Mahu. "You're driving as if possessed by Set, the god of chaos."

"I'm in no hurry, if truth be told," laughed Isis. "I just like driving fast and scaring people on the road. But you are right. I should slow down.

My father will be furious if I smash the oil jar."

She pulled on Neferu's reins and the donkey slowed down to a more sedate trot. The sun had fully risen by the time they reached the lake, where another market had been set up. Climbing down from the cart, Mahu thanked Isis. They all hugged the beautiful Neferu goodbye before setting off in search of their boat.

"I've been thinking," said Balaal, "what if we pass the vizier on the river? He might spot us."

"Fair point," replied Mahu. "We'll have to buy some disguises. But we need to be quick about it. I want to set sail as soon as possible."

Balaal spotted some wigs on a stall. "These will do," she said.

Renni looked at them in horror. "They're crawling with fleas."

"We'll dowse them in the river," laughed Balaal, paying for the wigs with a charm from her necklace. "The dirt in the water should kill any flea. And if we make some grand necklaces out of flowers, we'll look like rich people on our way back from a festival."

"You mean Renni and I will look like rich people," said Mahu, laughing. "You really *are* rich."

"I think you mean my father is rich," replied Balaal. "You'll find I only have a few charms left on my necklace. And only one last bangle, which I'm about to part with."

She paid the girl they'd left in charge of their boat. Renni looked around. The lake was full of boats. He wondered which one belonged to the vizier.

Above him, there was a familiar grunt. The ibis was sitting on the mast, its wings folded.

It seemed to be lost deep in thought.

14

Dance with the Crocodiles
- Mahu -

Even with all the fleas shaken out, the wigs were still itchy. And incredibly heavy on the head. Mahu couldn't understand why rich people insisted on wearing them. He'd even heard that some people put a lump of perfumed wax under their wig. It melted in the hot sun and ran down their necks, making them smell nice.

Mahu thought he'd rather stink than walk about feeling sticky and hot.

Still, the wigs and the garlands of flowers did their job. Most people they passed on the river mistook them for pilgrims returning from a festival.

"Had a good time?" they called across the

water. "Did the gods answer your prayers?"

"We had a great time, thank you," Mahu always replied, enjoying the attention. "The gods made all our wishes come true."

The ibis travelled with them, sometimes resting on the mast but most of the time flying on ahead, only to return. Mahu wondered if it would come with them all the way to Waset. Perhaps it would follow them home and his mother would tame it. Mahu's mother was very good with animals. This ibis would be a nice pet for her.

There was only one day left of the journey when Mahu spotted a large boat coming up behind them. Its deck was groaning under the weight of chests, jars and bales of linen. Two horses were tethered to the mast. *A trader*, thought Mahu. It had six rowers. Someone was busy going from one oarsman to another with a water jug.

Abanoub!

"That's Paser's boat," Mahu gasped. "I bet he's got his chariot hidden under those bales. He's travelling in disguise, like us. Row harder. We need to get to Waset before he does."

"And keep your heads down," warned Balaal. "We don't want him to spot us."

"May the gods help us," added Renni.

It seemed, though, that the gods were not listening that day. The vizier's boat crept closer and closer until the shadow of its sail fell across the deck of the children's boat.

One of the rowers called out. "Coming through! Make way! Make way!"

It made Mahu's blood boil. Why did owners of large boats always think they had right of way, as if they owned the river? Throwing caution to the wind, he called back:

"You make way if you want! We're staying where we are."

The rower was about to reply but someone who was sitting cross-legged on the deck raised a hand to stop him. He stood up, revealing a thin figure swathed in the colourful robes of a Northern trader. The disguise didn't fool Mahu. It was Paser. He smiled icily through the strands of a thick, brown wig.

"I apologise on behalf of my rude slave. He shouldn't talk to pilgrims like that, even if we do need to hurry home with our goods. I can tell by your garlands you have been to a festival."

Mahu could tell Paser was scrutinising him as he spoke. His eyes were narrowed in concentration.

"That we are, sir," said Mahu. His mind was racing as he spoke. He'd made a big mistake shouting at the rower. Had Paser remembered his voice?

"And was it a successful pilgrimage?" asked the vizier. "Did the gods answer all your prayers?"

"That they did, sir," replied Mahu, now keeping his eyes lowered. "All praise to them."

"And what wonderful festival are you returning from, may I ask?" Paser pressed him.

"Er," began Mahu, who had no idea what festivals were taking place at this time of the year.

He turned to Renni for help.

"We weren't at an actual festival as such," said Renni quickly, sweating under his own wig. "We just went to offer sacrifice to the great Isis in—"

"—in the city of Nubt," Mahu finished for him.

The vizier's eyes flashed and Mahu realised he'd made a mistake. He had no idea where Nubt was. If it was south of the river from Waset, then the vizier would realise they were lying. They were on the wrong stretch of the river. For all he knew, there might not even be a temple of Isis in Nubt.

Paser looked slowly from him to Renni to Balaal and the smile disappeared from his face. He reached inside his brightly coloured robes and drew out the was-sceptre.

"Greetings, my old friends," said the vizier with a chilling sneer. "I have been praying to Set that he might deliver you to me. You and I have an old score to settle, don't we?"

The was-sceptre's eyes started to flash an ember-bright red. "Look deep into the Set-animal's eyes, all three of you," commanded Paser. "Look deep... and fall under my spell."

Mahu felt his whole face going numb. Desperately, he tried to clear his head but the more he fought the was-sceptre's power, the stronger it seemed to get. It was like something was reaching into his heart, snuffing out his will.

"You three shall all dive into the river," he heard Paser say. "You shall dance with the crocodiles— your last, grisly dance."

Like a puppet pulled by strings, Mahu felt himself jerked to his feet. He looked over the side of the boat. Beneath the water's surface, enormous shadows trembled and circled. He thought he saw eyes, wide with evil hunger. Pointed teeth flashed. Were they real crocodiles, or magic ones conjured up by Paser?

"In the name of Set, I order you to jump, all three of you," ordered the vizier. "And may your *ka*s wander lost and desperate in the Duat forever."

Helpless to stop himself, Mahu lifted one foot over the side of the boat. He could see Renni and Balaal doing the same. Just then, a screeching sound cut through the fuzziness in his head. A flock of ibises was swooping down on the boat, their wings lashing out at the rowers. One of them made straight for Paser. It was their ibis, Mahu realised, and it knocked the was-sceptre out of the vizier's hand, sending it flying. It disappeared into the water with an angry hiss of steam.

His power over the children suddenly snatched away, Paser screamed with rage. Mahu's head cleared in an instant.

"Row!" he shouted at Renni and Balaal.

On his boat, the vizier grabbed hold of Abanoub by the shoulder.

"You," he screamed, his voice high with panic. "Get me back my was-sceptre." He hurled the boy overboard and turned to the rowers. "And the rest of you: help him! I don't care if most of you get eaten alive. I want the was-sceptre back."

The vizier pulled out a horse whip and started flailing at the poor rowers.

"That was a close one," said Balaal as they slipped away.

"I should learn to keep my mouth shut," said Mahu. He looked at Renni. His brother's eyes were fixed firmly on his oar.

"I'm sorry, Renni," he said.

But Renni didn't reply.

15

Mahu Meets Prince Khaem
- Renni -

Paser's boat had not caught up with theirs by the time Renni, Mahu and Balaal reached Waset and moored their boat. The water level was dropping. Renni could see the ring marks it had left on the tree trunks.

"I'm sorry, little brother," said Mahu, noticing how quiet Renni was.

"You nearly got us all killed," said Renni.

"I know," said Mahu. "Sometimes I don't think before I speak."

"But we're home safely now," said Balaal. "And that's the most important thing."

They walked away from the river in the

moonlight, the three of them lost deep in their own thoughts. It always amazed Renni how different he and Mahu were. Where Renni liked peace and quiet, Mahu preferred noise and merriment. While Renni chose to be mostly alone with his paints and brushes, Mahu always opted to be with a crowd of friends, having a good time. No doubt their chosen paths in life would take them away from each other; Mahu on the high seas, Renni deep in some tomb, painting. And yet they would be brothers for life.

"Balaal is right," Renni sighed. "The most important thing is that we're back in Waset safely. Let us speak no more about it. We should go and see the prince right away. You two must come with me."

"I'd love to come and help explain what we discovered," said Mahu, "but will the guards let me in?"

"I have the prince's ring," Renni reminded him. "I'm sure it will let us all in."

The palace guards had to confer with a senior officer when the three of them presented themselves at the main palace entrance. But soon the palace doors swung open and the children were told to wait for the prince in an ante-room.

"I thought Paser's house was luxurious," said Mahu, "but I never imagined riches like these existed, even in my wildest dreams." He pointed to a long seat covered in soft cushions. "Is that to sleep on?"

"Just to sit on," replied Renni. "When you are chatting with friends or reading a scroll."

"I suppose you are used to this kind of luxury," Mahu said to Balaal.

"My father's palace is nothing like Pharaoh's," replied Balaal hotly. "We of the Fenkhu believe in the richness of the inner spirit, not the palace and the temple."

A scowling servant in a blue loincloth and jangling necklaces led them into Prince Khaem's personal chamber, which seemed to have even more scrolls on the shelves than Renni remembered. The prince was looking at the stars from a huge window.

"My friend," he said, turning to Renni. "Welcome back."

"Thank you, Your Highness," replied Renni, bowing. "I do apologise for disturbing you late at night. I brought my brother and a friend with me because we have something very important to tell you. This is Balaal. She is a princess of the Fenkhu."

"A princess," said the prince, smiling at Balaal. "Forgive me, I was not told of your presence in our midst or I would have invited you to the palace."

"Don't worry, I am not in the Black Land as a princess, Your Highness," said Balaal. "I am here as a traveller to learn about the gods and the culture of your people."

"And this is my elder brother, Mahu," said Renni. Mahu bowed stiffly.

"You are all welcome," said Prince Khaem. "But you must be hungry even at this time of night. Can I offer you something to eat?"

"We'd rather discuss the urgent matter we came to talk to you about, Your Highness," said Renni. "We believe your life is in danger."

The prince's eyebrows rose. He indicated a seat. "Please, tell me more."

With help from Balaal and Mahu, Renni told the prince about their journey to Shedet. The prince's eyes widened when he heard about the vizier. "My father trusts Paser without question but I always suspected he was not the honest man he pretends to be. My spies in the palace tell me he is a powerful magician, and that he was after the same crocodile mummy I wanted. Thank Thoth I got there first."

"We were wondering why that mummy is so special?" asked Renni.

The prince smiled. "Come, let's find out."

16

The Crocodile Curse
- Renni -

The prince went to a corner of the room where a fire burnt in front of a statue of Thoth. He pressed the statue's toes and it swung back, revealing a secret door.

"I have a hidden room," explained the prince, "where I can study without being observed by other people's spies." He chuckled. "Everyone has spies in this palace, not just me. Even the spies here have spies. Which makes things very difficult: I can never be sure whether my spies are spying for me or *on* me."

He pulled open the secret door and, taking a lamp, descended a short flight of stairs. The others

followed him into a large room packed with the strangest collection of things.

Shelves groaned under the weight of carvings and statues rescued from ruined shrines and temples. There were rocks and pieces of glittering crystal. Animal bones hung like trophies on the walls.

"Oh look," said Balaal, stopping near a statue of a woman standing on a crescent moon. "Here's a carving of our own Fenkhu goddess, Astarte. She is the queen of the skies."

"I have lots of Fenkhu statues," said Prince Khaem proudly. "Some of them are very ancient. Sometimes I'm too scared to handle them, in case they crumble to dust in my hands. But look, here's the crocodile mummy from Shedet. I had not yet managed to find a moment to examine it."

He pointed to a mummy lying on a table. The binding was covered in fading pictures of cobras, matching the scrap of linen Paser had found in the mummy sanctuary.

"You may wonder what's inside this mummy," said Prince Khaem. "I think I know. The embalmers stuff the body with wads of papyrus to help keep its shape. Sometimes they use old documents they think are worthless. Marriage contracts, letters—that sort of thing." He stopped to relish the interested looks on his audience's faces. He had them in the palm of his hand. "And sometimes, someone might hide a very important document."

"And you think there is such a document in this mummy?" asked Renni.

"Perhaps," replied Prince Khaem. "A travelling storyteller from Waset recounted a story at one of my father's banquets. It was a strange tale of an ambitious magician who lived a long time ago. It is said that he was so powerful he could put spells on cobras to make them do his bidding. He was arrested for spying on behalf of an enemy plotting to overthrow the ruler of the time. Pharaoh's soldiers searched his house, trying to find a piece of writing, a message or a letter perhaps, that would prove his treason. Nothing was ever found.

"My guess is that the priest hid the papyrus inside this mummy. You see, no one would dare cut open a mummy. It is a crime against the land and the gods."

"How did Paser find out about it?" asked Mahu.

"He was present at the banquet," answered Khaem. "And, now that I think about it, he complained of food poisoning soon after. A clever trick to have us all thinking he was bed-ridden and not on a boat to Shedet."

"And why do you want the papyrus?" said Balaal.

"For my collection," replied the prince. "And, if it's dangerous, to keep it safe from anyone who might use it for the wrong purpose."

Renni looked at the mummy. In the faint light of the lamp, it seemed nothing more than a dead animal.

"Could there really be a dangerous secret inside it?" he thought out loud.

The prince smiled. "We're about to find out. Help me."

The three of them helped Prince Khaem turn the mummy over on its back, exposing its belly.

Prince Khaem held up his hands in prayer. "We ask the *ka* of this noble crocodile to forgive us for desecrating its mummy. We promise, in the name of Anubis, the lord of the dead, that we will make good our trespass. We shall restore it to its original state, and we shall offer sacrifice so that its *ka* might continue to enjoy its afterlife forever more. When we are done, we shall return it to its place of rest once more."

The prince took a knife and carefully made a neat cut down the mummy's belly. Renni half-expected worms and cockroaches to come crawling out but nothing like that happened. There wasn't even a bad or musty smell. The embalmers had done a good job.

Prince Khaem pulled the cut bandages aside, revealing the stuffing inside. He rifled through it carefully, pulling out one crumpled piece of papyrus after another. He handed each sheet to the others who smoothed them out. They were all blank.

Muttering to himself, the prince reached deeper into the mummy. "Ha," he said. "There is something here."

Carefully, he drew out a leather tube decorated with pictures of fish caught in a net. Renni felt the hairs on the back of his neck prickle. The colours were still as bright as the day the tube had been placed inside the mummy. He watched as the prince drew out a scroll and unrolled it.

Renni brought the lamp closer.

A SPELL TO CURSE AND TRAP A GOD!

The Myth of Set and Osiris
- Renni -

"A spell!" Renni looked up in horror. "Can someone really curse and capture a god?"

"According to legend, it's been done before," said Prince Khaem. "Mahu and Renni, you must know the story. The god Set dared his brother Osiris to climb inside a beautiful wooden chest. If he fit in it, Set promised Osiris could keep the chest. It was a devious trick, of course, because Set was angry that Osiris had been made king of the Black Land. The chest was really a coffin. With Osiris still inside, Set locked it and hurled it into the river."

"My tutor told me this story," said Balaal. "The

current swept the chest down the great river and out to open sea. One of our goddesses found it washed up on the shores of my own land."

"But that was a god capturing another god," said Renni. "Can a mortal like Paser do it?"

"Paser is a priest," said Balaal, "and, as we've seen, a powerful magician."

"Still," said Mahu. "Can he *really* capture a god?"

"Even the gods have feet of clay, it seems," said Prince Khaem. "With this spell, I think one can put a curse on a god. And if one of the gods is captured, it will unleash a terrible curse on the Black Land. It will throw the whole of the cosmos into chaos. It will upset the natural order of things." He rolled up the papyrus. "This is a very dangerous spell and if it falls into the wrong hands…" He shuddered. "I'm not sure it would be safe even locked in my secret room."

"There's only one thing to do," said Mahu.

The others turned to him.

"Destroy it," said Mahu. "Burn it. Now. No good

can come from keeping it."

"It pains me to destroy one single human thought," said the prince. "But… please, Renni, hand me the lamp."

Renni moved the lamp across the table and Prince Khaem held the papyrus to the flame. They all watched in silence as the edges started to curl and blacken.

But then there was an angry hiss. Someone leapt out of the shadows and snatched the burning papyrus out of Prince Khaem's hand.

It was Abanoub.

18

Paser
- Mahu -

The lamp fell to the floor and burning oil spread across the marble tiles. Mahu ripped off part of his tunic and swatted the flames, managing to smother them before they spread too far.

From the corner of his eye, he spotted Abanoub desperately trying to put out the flames on the scroll.

A figure stepped out of the darkness behind him. It snatched the scroll from his hands and wrapped the edges of a cloak around it, putting

out the flames.

"Paser," hissed Prince Khaem angrily. "How did you get in here? How did you even know about my secret room?"

The vizier chuckled. "What is it you said to your companions, Your Highness?" he sneered. "'Even the spies have spies in the palace.' But I do not need spies. I have a seeing-bowl. I can see anything in it."

"You and your slave are trespassing," thundered Prince Khaem. "I'm calling the guards."

"I wouldn't do that if I were you," said Paser calmly. With his free hand, he raised the was-sceptre with its glowing red eyes. "After all, they wouldn't be happy when you tell them that three commoners had broken into your private quarters… You'd be condemning your poor little friends to their deaths."

"I am not afraid of you or your spells," said Prince Khaem, although Mahu could detect a tremble in his voice now. "Look, I have an amulet of my own that protects me from your magic. Give me back that scroll. I order you as a prince of the royal household."

"I have every right to this spell," spat Paser, losing his composure for once. "I'm saving it from your idiotic destruction. Call yourself a scholar? Only ignorant fools destroy knowledge."

He poked Abanoub with the was-sceptre. "Come, wretch. We have work to do."

The vizier turned to Mahu, Renni and Balaal. "As for you lot, be sure that I'll seek you out again once I have put this spell to good use. And then, I'll put a curse on you too. You have meddled in my affairs for the last time."

Paser stepped back into the shadows, dragging Abanoub with him. A secret door slid open behind him and then closed again to hide them from view.

19

The Coming of Set

- Renni -

"We have to go after him," said Prince Khaem. "Help me." He rushed to the wall, trying to find the secret door. The others joined him, but no one could find so much as a crack in the plaster.

"Can't we go out another way?" asked Mahu. "You know, through the front door?"

"The prince can't just run out of the palace without permission from his father," said Renni. "And never without a guard to protect him."

"It's royal protocol," agreed Prince Khaem.

"And we don't even know where Paser is going," said Renni.

"Perhaps my goddess can help us with that,"

said Balaal. She hurried to the statue of Astarte and, putting her hand on it, closed her eyes. "Oh goddess, give me advice. Guide me. Tell me where we can find the wicked vizier?"

Renni saw Balaal's face twitch. Her eyelids flickered as she communed with her favourite goddess. A smile spread across her face and she nodded.

"The goddess showed me a wide avenue," she said, opening her eyes. "With two rows of sphinxes. And she showed me a temple with a feather carved above the door."

"The avenue of sphinxes is in Ipet-Isut," said Renni. "The Chosen of Places. It's a vast temple complex dedicated to many gods. I've been there with Uncle Pepy."

"And the feather belongs to Ma'at," said Prince Khaem. "Your goddess must mean Ma'at's temple at Ipet-Isut. You three must go there at once."

Mahu turned to the prince. "Forgive me if I am speaking out of turn, Your Highness. But you must come with us. Perhaps your amulet will protect us too. You can't think of royal protocol, whatever it is, at a time like this. Just come with us and walk straight past the guards without looking them in the eye. I bet they won't dare stop you."

Prince Khaem appeared to be deep in thought for a moment. Then, he said, "You are right. Let's go."

Renni could see a sparkle of excitement in the prince's eyes as he marched up the stairs and through the palace halls. Mahu was right. Not one single guard dared stop them. It was still dark as they left the palace. The sky was peppered with stars. Renni caught sight of the ibis, wheeling high in the air. He hoped it was following them to Ipet-Isut. It would be a comfort, knowing it was there, should they need help.

Renni felt fear spread through his veins as he thought of what might lie ahead. Once again, he was having to face grave danger. How could they, just children, defeat a powerful vizier?

A little voice whispered in his head. *But you did*

it before. You and your brother…

Yes, me and my brother, thought Renni. He looked at Mahu running on ahead, leading the group and hungry for action. *I might be the artist, thought Renni, but Mahu is the brave one. I need him more than he needs me.*

When they reached the temple, the guards bowed at Prince Khaem and opened the gate. Inside, the complex was as silent as a grave, the moon shining on empty columns and walkways.

Prince Khaem held up a hand as they approached Ma'at's temple. A guard was at the door, his sword swinging lazily from his hand.

"He's asleep on his feet," whispered Mahu. "Look, his eyes are wide open."

"Paser must have put a spell on him with that sceptre of his," said Balaal. "That means he is in there."

They stole past the snoring guard into a large hall surrounded by pillars. They hid behind one of them and peered out. A huge statue of Ma'at stood at the far end with an altar beneath it. A fire-pit glowed nearby.

Paser was standing at the altar, his back to the children. He held the was-sceptre in his hand.

A coffin, painted in garish red, lay on the altar. "Open it, you fool, open it," Paser barked to Abanoub. The boy, head bowed, lifted the coffin lid.

Balaal whispered to Mahu and Prince Khaem. "What do we do now?"

"We wait until the vizier pulls out the scroll," said the prince.

"Yes," said Mahu. "And, when I give the signal, we all rush him and one of us grabs it. There's four of us and only two of them. We should be able to do it."

"And then we all run out of the temple in different directions," said Balaal. "That will confuse them."

Paser held up the was-sceptre. He muttered a spell and a red mist started to pour out of its glowing eyes. It took the shape of a strange creature, part jackal and part donkey.

"That's the Set-animal," gasped Renni. "Set's messenger."

The Set-animal undulated and floated above the vizier, like a deadly snake toying with a petrified mouse. "*Paser, you have summoned me.*"

"I summoned your master," replied the vizier. "He and I have an agreement."

"*The Master is busy*," hissed the Set-animal. "*You will have to be content with talking to me. Rest assured, I will convey your message.*"

"I spoke with your master in my seeing-bowl,"

replied the vizier. "I have the spell to trap a god. He said that if I do it, he will help me achieve my greatest ambition."

"*You want to become a god yourself,*" said the Set-animal.

Behind the pillar, Renni's blood ran cold. The vizier, a god. It was unthinkable. There would be no stopping his evil if his wish came true.

"*You are the master's revenge on the other gods,*" growled the Set-animal. "*Those who sided with his brother Osiris in the battle for the throne of the Black Land at the beginning of time. When you trap the goddess, the whole order of life will collapse. The gods will lose their power. The river will flood but only to drown and kill. The sun will not rise. Without the gods' protection, enemies will invade the Black Land. Chaos and terror will prevail. Set, the god of disorder, will reign supreme.*"

"And I will reign beside him," shouted Paser, his eyes wild at the thought of so much power. "We shall be an alliance forged in hate and anger."

"Get on with the spell, Paser," boomed the Set-animal.

Paser let go of the was-sceptre and it remained standing, as if held by invisible hands. He pulled the scroll out of his robe and read it aloud.

"To curse and capture a god, I invite ye the stars to shake the heavens, ye the moon to weep tears of blood. Let them fill the sacred river. I order ye, wind, to blow the sand of hate…"

"Now, before he reads anymore!" hissed Mahu, as a hot wind started to blow through the temple doorway. He, Prince Khaem and Balaal leapt out from behind the pillar. Renni was about to follow but the was-sceptre turned in their direction. The red eyes glowed. There was a flash of red lightning and Mahu, Balaal and the prince stopped dead in their tracks, as if invisible hands were holding them back. The sceptre had proved too strong for the prince's amulet. It had put them under a spell.

Immersed in reading the scroll, the vizier did not even glance at them. He continued reciting,

"By the power of the first *ka*, the first day, the first night, I invoke ye earth to tremble…"

Held fast by fear, Renni felt the ground shake under his feet.

"I invoke stone and marble to come alive…"

The temple seemed to groan and the great statue of Ma'at trembled. Clouds of dust rose from it. Chunks of marble cascaded to the floor. The statue cracked in two, like an egg releasing a chick. A golden mist, full of light, plumed out of it. It took the shape of a woman with a feather on her head.

Ma'at!

The goddess opened her eyes. For a moment, a smile played on her face, but then Paser's voice got louder.

"I invoke ye, wind, to capture this goddess, to curse her, to bind her in unbreakable chains…"

The spell started to take effect on the goddess. She was dragged, as if by invisible chains, towards the open coffin. Her hands raked at the air. A silent

160

shriek came out of her mouth.

Renni realised what Paser was doing. It was the story of Set and Osiris all over again, except this time it was Ma'at who was about to be trapped in a coffin. And that's when something inside Renni snapped. He had to do something, to save the goddess, to save his friends. And his brother!

Cautiously, Renni stole out from behind the pillar. Out of the corner of his eye, he saw Abanoub crouching in the shadows. The boy nodded at him, urging him on. He forced himself to creep closer and closer, past the was-sceptre whose glowing eyes remained fixed on the other three children.

The vizier was still reading, his voice now bellowing. **"Chains of wrath, tie the goddess down fast, coffin contain her..."**

And then, Renni pounced and snatched the scroll from Paser's hands. The vizier roared with fury. The was-sceptre flew back into his hands and he turned it on Renni.

"By the power of Set, I command you…"

Renni felt himself choking. His muscles began to freeze even as his grip tightened on the scroll.

"Help!" A strangled scream came out of his mouth. "Help!"

With his head bent backwards by the power of the sceptre, Renni saw the ibis swoop in through a window. He had the impression that the eyes were human again and this time he recognised them.

"General Tatia!"

The ibis shot like an arrow towards Paser. In a whirl of feathers, it transformed into the general's *ka*. The vizier hit out blindly with the was-sceptre but Tatia snatched it out of his grasp.

He leapt away with it.

"Help me," Paser screamed at the Set-animal.

The creature only hissed angrily. Something was holding it back from leaping to Paser's rescue. The feathers whirled around Tatia again and a moment later, he had turned back into an ibis. An ankh shone brightly on its forehead like a medal, a badge of honour. It swooped up in the air, the was-sceptre clasped firmly in its beak.

With his sceptre out of reach, Paser's power seemed to vanish.

The Set-animal pulsated with rage. Ma'at's ankh had prevented it from helping the vizier.

"*Pathetic mortal. You have wasted my master's time.*" It disappeared in a burst of angry flames.

Renni felt his muscles relax. He could move, he could breathe. Behind him, Mahu, Balaal and Prince Khaem were also released from the was-sceptre's spell.

"You, child, give me back that scroll!" Paser demanded, his hands outstretched.

Renni shook his head. "No."

"I said give it to me!"

"Give it to you… or what?"

"By the power of Set…" growled Paser.

Renni thrust the spell into the fire pit.

"No! You fool!" howled Paser, leaping at the fire. But it was too late. The scroll blackened against the glowing embers and turned to ashes.

The burning of the magic words released Ma'at from Paser's incomplete spell. She flew swiftly to her feet. Her hand plucked the ostrich feather from her hair. A loud whisper escaped her lips.

"I know that your heart would weigh more than this feather, follower of Set. Let's test your magic against the power of the gods."

She pointed the feather at Paser. The invisible chains that had trapped the goddess now wrapped themselves around him. They dragged him, kicking and spitting towards the coffin and he stumbled backwards into it.

"Help me, boy!"

Answering his master's call, Abanoub leapt out of his hiding place. Only this time, Renni noticed his eyes were not full of fear. Instead, they were shining with mischief.

Abanoub leapt at the coffin and slammed the lid down, trapping his master inside. The goddess smiled. She turned to the children and raised her feather in blessing. Another whisper echoed around the children's heads.

"Thank you, all of you! You have been extremely brave. You have saved the Black Land. You have

saved the gods themselves. When it is your turn to face Anubis and the scales of justice, your actions today will help your hearts weigh lighter than my feather." Ma'at looked up at the ibis still perched on a window high up in the temple. *"And thank you, General Tatia. The children could not have done this without your help."*

The ibis nodded its head in salute and flew out of the window, taking the was-sceptre with it. The first rays of the morning sun shone through the open doorway, dispersing the golden mist: Ma'at was gone.

The children were silent for a long while, thinking about all that had happened. Voices from outside interrupted their thoughts. Worshippers had arrived for the first ritual of the day.

Renni turned to the coffin where the vizier was thumping furiously on the lid. "Let me out! I order you under pain of death! Let me out!"

"Let him shout," said Prince Khaem, signalling to the temple guard who had also been released from the was-sceptre's spell. "He shall never bother or threaten anyone again, I promise you. He will be locked away in a place from which he can never return."

Renni indicated Abanoub who was watching them from the altar. "And what will happen to him?"

"He is the vizier's accomplice," said Prince Khaem. "He will be punished."

"But he could have stopped me from snatching the scroll out of Paser's hands," said Renni, "and he didn't. I don't think Abanoub can be considered Paser's accomplice."

"My brother is right," said Mahu. "Abanoub was under Paser's control."

"And he definitely redeemed himself by locking the vizier into the coffin," said Balaal.

"Perhaps you have a point," said the prince. "The boy has indeed been brave. He deserves a chance to explain himself."

He turned to the altar but Abanoub was not there. Renni peered at the shadows, hoping to find him, but it seemed he had managed to slip away. Renni wondered, with both a flutter of hope and a pang of worry, whether he'd ever see the boy again.

"Come, my friends," said Prince Khaem as priests filed into the temple, carrying incense and flowers for Ma'at. "That adventure has given me a great appetite. It's breakfast time. I invite you all to come back to the palace."

Following the prince, Renni thought of the fantastic pictures he and Uncle Pepy had painted. The adventure he'd just had was almost like he had fallen into one of them. It would be a great story to paint. A lowly painter helping to save the world, to save the gods themselves. But who would believe it? It sounded like a legend, a myth of old.

But the best bit of the story, thought Renni, *is that I proved to myself that I have courage. I helped save my brother and my friends. Until now, Mahu has always been the one to protect me.*

Today I protected him.

Epilogue

The god-judges were assembled in a circle once more. Their golden eyes twinkled like stars around General Tatia again. His dog, who had been patiently waiting for its master in the Duat, whined happily.

Anubis appeared with the scales of justice. The general's heart, flashing like a gemstone, sat in one pan. The other was empty, waiting.

Ma'at appeared in a shower of light. Her eyes shone brighter than all other gods. A smile crossed her lips as she took the was-sceptre from the general's hand. The goddess whispered and the sceptre crumbled into a shower of rose petals that swirled towards the Black Land far below.

"We are assembled today," she announced to the other gods, "because we had a dilemma, a problem. You weighed the general's heart against my feather and their weight was equal. His good and noble deeds did not outweigh his selfish ones. So, should the general's ka be welcomed into the blessed Field of Reeds, or should it be fed to the monster Ammut? I proposed a solution. Give the general one last test and let that decide."

"He did well," called out Nosey One. "He helped the very ones who had once caused him pain and grief. That shows he can forgive."

"He turned himself into a lowly bird and that shows humility," added Flame.

"He did much more than help the children," cut in You-of-the-Darkness. "He helped the children save us, the very gods who rule over the Black Land."

"Ah, but perhaps his goal was to save his ka, not to help others or save us," said the Pale One.

"We shall see if the general's actions have saved his ka," said Ma'at. She removed the ostrich feather from her hair and placed it on the scales of justice. General Tatia watched, breathless, as it slowly weighed down the pan. Down... down... slowly down...

The general's dog whined happily. At last, the pan with Ma'at's feather hung lower than the one with his master's heart.

"Well done, general," said Ma'at. "You have saved me and, with me, the harmony and wellbeing of the universe. You deserve to go straight to the Field of Reeds. Follow me. Your loved ones await."

The general and his dog watched in awe as a pearly gate opened behind the goddess. They saw familiar faces waiting, smiling, and together they stepped into the glorious Field of Reeds.

The End

Renni, Mahu and Balaal's
adventures continue in

THE
JACKAL'S
GRAVEYARD

GLOSSARY
& AUTHOR NOTES

Aaru • The Ancient Egyptian's version of heaven or paradise. They called it the Field of Reeds or the Field of Rushes. According to ancient texts there were seven gates that led to it but I have only used one in the story.

Amulet • A lucky charm, sometimes worn in a sidelock or as another piece of jewellery, like a pendant, a bangle or a ring.

Beautiful Festival of the Valley • A festival honouring the dead. It was held every year in the city of Waset.

Black Land • The Ancient Egyptians' name for their country. It was inspired by the rich, dark soil along the River Nile.

Cinnamon • A rich and expensive spice made from the bark of trees.

Double Crown of the Black Land • For a long time, Egypt was actually two kingdoms: Upper and Lower Egypt. When they were united, long before the time our story is set, Pharaoh started wearing a double crown. It showed he ruled over both Lower and Upper Egypt.

Duat • The underworld! A horrible, dark place where some of the gods lived.

Fenkhu • A word that described an ancient people today known as the 'Phoenicians'. Their descendants are the people of Lebanon.

Iteru • The Ancient Egyptian name for the Nile. It means simply 'the river'.

Ka • A part of the soul, or spirit, that survived after a person's death.

Kemet • The Ancient Egyptian word for Egypt.

Mut • Mother.

Papyrus • A material very much like thick writing paper. It is made from parts of the papyrus plant.

Pharaoh • The ruler of Ancient Egypt.

Sarcophagus • A stone coffin. The plural is 'sarcophagi'.

Scroll of Coming Forth By Day • Also known as the Book of the Dead. It was a long piece of writing that explained to people how to get to the Field of Reeds.

Set-animal • A strange fictional creature, unlike any real animal, living or extinct. It was the symbol of the god Set.

Sesh Qedut • An apprentice, someone who is still learning their trade.

Sidelock • A lock of hair growing on one side of the head.

Was-sceptre • A stick with an animal head and a double point at the bottom. It was a symbol of power, often seen carried by gods in pictures.

Yam • The Phoenician god of water.

ANCIENT EGYPTIAN GODS

Assessors of Ma'at • The Assessors of Ma'at were forty-two gods responsible for judging souls of the dead in the afterlife. They each had individual names and wrongdoings to assess.

Horus • Horus was the god of the sky and kingship. He had the head of a falcon, and was the son of Osiris and Isis and the nephew of Set.

Knut • Also known as Nut. She was the sky goddess and mother of Osiris, Isis, Set and Nephthys.

Ptah • The god of creation and maker of things. He was said to look after sculptors and architects.

Thoth • The god of writing and learning. He was often shown as a man with the head of an ibis.

LOCATIONS

Shedet, the city of crocodiles, is the oldest city in Egypt. Famous for its crocodile temples, it lay in an oasis south of modern-day Cairo. Ancient Greek and Roman writers called it Crocodilopolis. Founded around 4000BC, today it is called Fayum.

Ipet-Isut was a vast and important temple complex, part of the city of Luxor and one of the biggest sacred places in the world. Its name means 'Chosen of Places'.

Built over a long period of time, it had temples and buildings dedicated to Mont, the god of war, Mut, the goddess-wife of Amun-Ra and—most dazzling of all—the temple of Amun-Ra himself.

Archaeologists believe the outer walls were once surrounded by wonderful palaces and gardens. None of these buildings remain but the temple ruins make Ipet-Isut the second most visited site in Egypt after the pyramids in Giza.